The Life and Faith
of
Art Anderson

By: Art Anderson

Order this book online at www.trafford.com
or email orders@trafford.com

Most Trafford titles are also available at major online book retailers.

Note for Librarians: A cataloguing record for this book is available from Library
and Archives Canada at www.collectionscanada.ca/amicus/index-e.html

Printed in Victoria, BC, Canada.

Photo credit: Rogers Photography

ISBN: 978-1-4251-6113-2

*We at Trafford believe that it is the responsibility of us all, as both individuals
and corporations, to make choices that are environmentally and socially sound.
You, in turn, are supporting this responsible conduct each time you purchase a
Trafford book, or make use of our publishing services. To find out how you are
helping, please visit www.trafford.com/responsiblepublishing.html*

*Our mission is to efficiently provide the world's finest, most comprehensive
book publishing service, enabling every author to experience success.
To find out how to publish your book, your way, and have it available
worldwide, visit us online at www.trafford.com*

Trafford rev. 6/29/2009

 www.trafford.com

North America & international
toll-free: 1 888 232 4444 (USA & Canada)
phone: 250 383 6864 ♦ fax: 250 383 6804 ♦ email: info@trafford.com

CONTENTS

.

PREFACE

This is not a "tell -all" book. Nevertheless, as most families are to some degree, my family was dysfunctional. However, I am not going to dwell on the negative acts and faults of others in order to put a halo over my own head. I, too, have faults and have made grievous mistakes.

This is a book about my life and my faith. It is a book about the history of my family; about life in Kentucky on a rural family farm in the 1940's and 50's; one and two-room rural elementary schools and country churches.

The most valuable aspects of my young life were the religious training and teaching that I received. It is something that I would not exchange for the whole world. I wish it had been better than it was and I know of other children that received far better.

The things that I have done during my life that were good, I am indebted to others—most of whom have departed this life in body but not in spirit. My faults and shortcomings are my responsibility. Therefore, I will not try to justify my faults and failures by blaming others.

The social sciences teach that we are products of our childhoods. There was psychological harm inflected upon me when I was a child that has followed me all of my life and will continue to follow me for the remainder of my life. I wish I could understand why many of the harmful things were done. I cannot. I have wrestled with these demons for years and I do not have an answer.

Many of the negative and unpleasant experiences of my life

will be omitted which relate to my family and others whom I have no desire to hurt or to offend their relatives who are still living. However, a few things need to be exposed for history and educational purposes. Words and deed can hurt and do a lot of damage for a very, very long time. Once something is done, it cannot be undone. Causes do have effects. There have been events in my life that I do not discuss with anyone. God knows it all, and some things I do not understand. I am resolved to the fact that I shall never understand it all.

My dad was sixty-one years old when I was born. Men in their sixties are too old to start young families. And when they are in the seventies and eighties, they are too old to deal with teenagers. I never had a meaningful conversation with my dad in my life and neither did my six years' older brother.

There were three male figures that had the most influence on me during my growing-up years. They were my uncle Addie Anderson; my brother-in-law, Ray Chrisman; and my brother, Orvis. My brother spent far more time with me than any of the others. I have often said that I feel like I was child reared by a child. I feel that I was truly short-changed in life; however, it could have been far worse. On the other hand, I feel that I was extraordinarily blessed by the wonderful religious training that I was exposed to and the positive influence that others in the community had on my life.

This book is not intended to be a book of condemnations or fault finding. However, the truth will dictate that it be some of both. It is intended to be an educational book regarding social, cultural, history, and religious matters.

The first seven chapters are about my life. The remaining chapters are about my faith in God. My goal was to write a book that is simple, streamlined, easy to understand, a fast read, that is sufficiently complete that those unexposed to a church going life can understand the reality of God and his love for mankind, and show the relationship that God seeks with his creation.

Mankind must accept God at his word by faith.

Nevertheless, there are historical events recorded in the Holy Bible and history which, I believe, ascertain the existence of an all powerful and all knowing God. Those who seek him and desire to live righteous lives according to his will, will in due time be rewarded. God is also a God of judgment and sin has never and never will go unpunished. God's condemnation of sin applies to individuals, nations, and the world. My goal has been to make these truths plain and simple to understand— from both a biblical and historical point of view.

I hope it is not disappointing.

Art Anderson
November, 2007

PART ONE
MY LIFE

CHAPTER ONE

YOUNG LIFE

I was born in the small, rural community of Ono, in Russell County, Kentucky, on the 31st day of December 1943, to Marsillus and Lula Anderson, in an old two-story white weather-boarded farm house. The house, as originally constructed, was known as a "boxed" house. A "boxed" house was one built of double layers of lumber. This house also had a third layer on the inside of tongue- and-grooved lumber. When it was originally built, it was a two-room—two-story house. However, it had been remodeled by adding a third room for the kitchen and painted white. It had originally been heated by a fireplace, but by the time I was born, it was heated with a sheet-iron, wood-burning stove, and lit with kerosene lamps. Neither electric nor telephone service was available until years later. My mother cooked on a wood-burning cooking stove; washed our clothes on a washboard, and raised most of our food. She canned and dried a lot of our food for the winter months.

In addition to my parents, the family consisted of my brother, Orvis, whom were six years older than I by a few days; my grandmother, Talitha Anderson (1856—1945) whom died a few days prior to my second birthday. I also had an older half-brother and a half-sister.

My dad had been married prior to marrying my mother. His first wife and mother of my two half-siblings was Sarah

Luettia Wilson of Pulaski County, Kentucky. Sarah Luettia was the daughter of Aaron (1861–1936) and Margaret (1862–1931) Wilson. They were married on the fifth day of August 1906. Dad was twenty-three years old and Sarah was twenty-two. During their marriage, they lived near her family in Pulaski County. Luettia died of tuberculosis (T.B.) on the seventh day of April 1931, twelve years after they were married. When she died, their son, Carson, (1907-82) was eleven-years-old, and their daughter, Eskay, (1911-93) was seven.

Carson married Eva Ada Rexroad (1911-95) of the Salem community of Russell County and they had one daughter, Mary Magdalene. Eskay married Edward Ray Chrisman and had no children.

After Luettia died, dad took his two children and moved back to his mother's home in Russell County and was living there when he married my mother and his mother lived with my parents until her death nine years' later.

My dad was born on the Seventh day of September 1882, and was sixty-one years old at my birth. My mother was born on the 28th day of September 1905, and was thirty-eight years old at my birth. My dad had one brother. Addie Elmer, whom was born on the 16th day of February 1880; and two sisters, one of whom, Venettie, was married to Rev. Joe L. Wooldridge, an old-time circuit riding preacher.

Rev. Wooldridge would be gone from home for weeks and months at a time preaching revivals. It was, in fact, Rev. Woodridge that introduced my mom and dad. Dad lived in Russell County and mom in Wayne County and the counties were separated by the Cumberland River. They dated for two or three years via letters and an occasional visit by dad. They were married when dad was fifty-three years old and mom was thirty-two.

My dad's brother, Addie Elmer, always known as "Addie," had married Ollie Wilson and they had one daughter, Geneva (1908–10). She died at the age of two from injuries of a fire. She lived two weeks after the accident.

Russell County was a fairly popular place in the early part

of the twentieth century because the Cumberland River flowed along its southern border and served as a steamboat route for the southern and southeastern parts of the state. One of the popular boats was the famous Rowenna, which went up the river to Burnside.

Burnside is most famous for the founding of the first Boy Scouts. Before the Boy Scouts of America was organized in 1910, a troop of fifteen was formed in Burnside in 1908 by Mrs. Myra Greeno Bass using the official handbook of English scouting.

It has also served the timber and hardwood lumber industry for many years. It is home to one of the nation's top producers of hardwood flooring, and one of Kingsford's charcoal manufacturing facilities. It uses tens of thousands of tons of sawdust and coal each year making charcoal. Around 1950 the Cumberland River was flooded by the building of the Wolf Creek Dam, and Burnside became famous for what the locals call the *Ohio Navy*—residents of Ohio who come with their large sport boats to fish, ski, vacation, and party on Lake Cumberland.

My dad was just a poor dirt farmer. He owned a hundred-acre farm, which he had gotten by buying his siblings' shares after his father, Shelby Anderson (1849—1919), died. It lay on Ono Ridge between the waters of Wolf and Caney Fork creeks. He did not raise a lot of products—a few acres of corn, an acre of tobacco, and a few acres of hay. He still did a lot of hard work when I was small. He only had a pair of mules with which to work the farm. He always had milk cows and raised a couple of hogs for our meat. For years when I was very small, they skimmed the cream off the milk and sold it once or twice a week to a local lady, Roxie Popplewell, who had a "cream station." They also had a small flock of chickens, from which they sold eggs. Basically, the family's income was from sales of cream, eggs, tobacco, and periodically a calf. The family's income in the 1940's was perhaps less than fifteen hundred dollars per year.

When I was born, dad owned a 1924 Model T Ford automobile.

3

I do not remember very much about the car. He sold it when I was very small. It had not been driven for perhaps twenty years. He never owned another car in his life. He did not have a tractor until he brought a new International Harvester, Super A, in May 1950. Until then he had done all of his work with a pair of mules, Lou and Liz.

My mother was the daughter of Frank Henderson Parmley (1878–1960) and Josie (Spradlin) Parmley (1884–1957). My mother could trace her roots all the way back to when one of her ancestors—then a small boy—had boarded a boat in Ireland and looked back at his footprints in the sand and said to himself that "that they would be the last tracks he would ever make in Ireland." And, indeed, they were.

My mother had eight brothers and one sister. Her brothers were Miles (1903–1978)—always known as "Bill"; Clyde (1912–1988), Everette (1918–1967) Hager, Fred; and Vernie, James "Jimmy," and Elmer. Vernie, James and Elmer all died while they were children. She had one sister, Lilly, whom was ten years younger that she. Her brothers were all farmers and carpenters, and they and their children have built some of the better homes in Wayne County. Mills was also a Baptist minister and pastured a church in Wayne County for many years.

My mother spent very little time with her family after marrying dad. One of the reasons was the impounding of Wolf Creek Dam. Transportation was not a small problem. The families were only six or eight miles apart via horse-back, but when the lake came in it was a seventy mile drive. Therefore, I spent very little time with my grandparents on my mother's side and my grandfather on my father's side was already deceased when I was born, and I do not remember my dad's mother at all. I can only remember seeing my grandfather a couple of times and my grandmother once.

When I was young, we attended the Square Oak church located on the Somerset-Jamestown Road in the Ono community. The church derived its name from an oak tree in its yard that was once nearly square because someone had nailed four boards around it and as it grew it became nearly square. As of this writing, the tree is still there but its square shape is almost gone.

The center of the community was the "crossroads"; the area where the Somerset-Jamestown Road intersected with the Ono Ridge Road. A country store sat on one corner, the elementary school on another, an old grist mill building sat on another, and an old dilapidated store building was on the other corner. The church was located a couple of hundred yards from the crossroads on the Somerset-Jamestown Road to the east.

From the time I can remember, the church was an older building but in a good state of repair. When I was small, I remember it had two kerosene lamps that hung from the ceiling and was heated by a sheet-iron stove. Later it had electric lights and was heated by a fuel-oil stove. My dad helped build it. Before it was built, religious services in the community were held sporadically in the woods in what was called *brush harbor* meetings. I have heard my dad tell about going down on the creeks and taking up collections of eggs to buy the nails and pay for having the lumber sawed to build the church. The land where the church was situated had been donated by Mark Wilson. Mr. Wilson was a brother of my Uncle Addie's wife, Ollie. The deed stipulated that the church was to be free for all denominations except Mormons and Catholics.

When the church building was relatively new it was bombed with dynamite. According to my uncle Addie, some of the local bootleggers and moon-shiners were angry because they believed that some of the church-goers had been informing the local law enforcement about their illegal liquor activities. One night near the time of the bombing of the church, the late Oscar Higginbotham was shot in the leg as he was walking home from church, allegedly by one of the local illegal moon-shiners and bootleggers.

During my early years, I never knew of but two groups using the building. One was the Missionary Baptists and the other was the Separate Baptists. From my earliest memory, there were a lot of animosities between the two congregations. The controversy between the two groups was predicated on the doctrine of eternal salvation held by the Missionaries, and the Separate Baptists held a different view. My parents were members of the Missionary Baptists; my half-sister was a member of the Separate Baptists.

Sharing the building as the two groups did, each of the respective pastors came for services only once per month. One of the groups held their pastoral services on a Saturday afternoon or evening and the following Sunday morning, and the other group held theirs on a different Saturday afternoon or evening and the following Sunday morning. Therefore, there was a preaching service on two Sundays per month. The two groups jointly held Sunday school every Sunday morning. Each of the groups held a revival once per year. Revival services were held at 10:00 a.m. on weekdays and after Sunday school on Sundays, and at 6:00 or 7:00 p.m.

Revival services were generally held during the school year. When a revival was in progress, the teachers would march the students to the church for the morning service. After the services, we would march back to the school for lunch and the afternoon classes.

Several families in the community did not attend church on Sundays. The only times their children were ever in church were during the revivals. Some of those children professed faith in Christ years later.

When the preachers came for the monthly services or to the revivals, they spent the night or nights with a member of the congregation. By my time, most of the preachers had cars, but in earlier times they had ridden horses or had come by bus. Some of the old time preachers that I remember spending nights with us were preachers Kimbler and Walter Compton of Adair County, and an elderly preacher and his son, the Bradleys, of Casey County. Their home church built a new building in the Windsor community in Casey County and named it *Bradley's Pleasure* because the elder Bradley loved the church and the community so much and had served as its pastor for many years.

My half-sister, Eskay, and Ray Chrisman lived on Caney Fork creek before the dam was built. They had a large farm on the creek that Ray had gotten from his parents, William and Mary Chrisman. I can remember being at their home only one time. The dam was coming in and they were preparing to relocate to Jamestown. Ray had siblings, one brother, Marion, and one sister Mollie. He had gotten the creek farm from his parents because his parents were on the "outs" with his brother Marion. Marion and Esto Dunbar had robbed and killed Mary Chrisman's father—Marion's grandfather—Elmer Eastham on March 13, 1942, at that time Marion was thirty-seven years old. They had placed his body in the road with the hope and intent that Elmer's son, Willard, would run over him with his vehicle on his way home from work and be blamed for his father's death. Willard didn't run over his father's body. The murderers were charged and went to prison for a few years. Ray had a passionate dislike for his brother Marion for the rest of his life. There was a friendly but strained relationship between the Chrismans and the Easthams.

In his younger years, Ray had also killed a man. He was a Coffey, reared on Concord Ridge in Russell County. Ray claimed that the trouble came up over Coffey stealing his chickens. Others said that Ray and his brother Marion as well as Coffey were making moonshine liquor and Ray and Marion wanted all the business and falsely accused Coffey of stealing his chickens. Ray and Coffey were at a revival that was being conducted by Rev. Joe Wooldridge and Coffey was outside the church with a shotgun under his overcoat and was going fox hunting after service. Ray's brother Marion was there, too, and went inside the church and told Ray that Coffey was outside the church with a shotgun and was going to kill him and gave Ray his pistol. When the service ended, Ray took a few steps toward the front door of the church and stepped upon a bench and shot Coffey. Ray was indicted for the murder, on the twenty-eighty day of October 1924 and found not guilty on the eighteenth day of June 1925 by a Russell County Circuit Court jury. The late James C. Carter was the presiding judge. Ray was represented by the late Josh Chumbley. Mr. Chumbley was a well known and respected practicing lawyer; however, he had never attended law school.

When the dam was about to be built, the federal government took Ray and Eskay's creek farm and they brought a grocery store in Jamestown and operated it until they retired.

Eskay was weakly and sick a lot of the time. Dad would go to their home and help Ray cut his tobacco, harvest his hay, and cut wood, etc.

When I was very small, I remember going to the corn fields with mom and dad to harvest the corn—they called it "gathering corn"—and it would take half-day of a day to pick a wagon load. When the weather was wet, they would go to the barn and strip tobacco—that is pull the leaves off of the stalks--and tie the leaves into what they called "hands" and then it was ready to go to market. In the fall, after the tobacco was cut and in the barns, but before it was ready to strip and the corn was ready to harvest, dad and Uncle Addie would cut firewood for our winter's heating and cooking. They used the brush from the woodcutting for fuel to burn the next year's tobacco's plant bed. That was how they tried to kill the weed seeds in the ground. They way my dad farmed, it was a lot of hard work.

In February or March, he would burn the plant bed, generally 100 feet long by 9 feet wide. They he and mom would dig the bed up with hoes and work the soil with garden rakes until it was suitable for sowing the seeds. He would mix the tobacco seeds with corn meal, because tobacco seeds are very, very small, and sow them. Then they would cover the bed with canvas to protect the seeds and young plants until a couple of weeks before the plants were big enough to transplant to the field. When the plants were large enough to withstand the stress of transplanting, and the ground was wet, they would pull the plants and transplant them in the field. One would drop the plants on the ground and others would follow and set them into the ground.

For the time I was small until I was in my teens, my dad, my brother or I would plow the tobacco with a mule and a three-shovel plow. We plowed the corn with the three-shovel and a two-shovel (double-shovel) plows.

Then came the worming—walking over the entire field each morning and getting the worms off the tobacco—hoeing, spraying, and later topping, suckering, and finally the cutting and housing until time to strip it and get it to market.

Much of the way that dad farmed was unique by the community standards at that time. The other farmers of the community did not do the worming and hoeing like dad and we kids did. The others in the community didn't necessary have tractors in the earliest of times, but they did things in a more modern fashion than dad did and with less hard work. Dad and mom did things back then very much like the Amish farm today.

CHAPTER TWO

DADDY'S LITTLE HELPER AND OTHER MISCHIEVOUS DEEDS

When I was not at school or out playing, I was around dad and Uncle Addie. Addie was at our home working a lot, and also on Sunday afternoons. Many times he and dad would walk to the lake or back in the fields or to a neighbor's home for a visit. I generally was tagging along with them.

Therefore, I always knew what their plans were for the forthcoming days. It was becoming hay cutting time and dad had mentioned that he was going to put some new rivets in his mowing machine. I was probable six or seven years' old. I remember it was before he got the tractor.

I got his box of rivets, and in my bare feet, and with my bib coveralls and straw hat on, I went out to the barn and looked over the old mower. For the life of me, I could not locate where in the rivets went. I decided that the only place they could go were in the gear box. Somehow, I got the oil filler cap off and put the whole box of rivets in the gear box. I was very proud of my little self!

A few days later, dad got to looking for the box of rivets and couldn't find them. I reared back and proudly announced that I had already put them in the machine. Dad didn't buy that! He questioned me about where I had put them. I proudly told him. He was angry to put it mildly. Mom thought it was funny. Dad didn't say too much. He would go get Uncle Addie to help him get them out.

They tried to get the mower out of the barn in order to better see. The wheels wouldn't roll, just scoot. It took Uncle Addie and dad a full afternoon to get the gear box apart and the rivets out.

Dad always kept a block of salt out for the livestock. It came in fifty pounds' blocks. The cows and mules had eaten all of it and were out. Dad mentioned something about getting them some. I, as usual, was listening and came up with an instant solution!

I believed that the mules needed some salt right-a-way. I went into the smokehouse and got some salt that dad had used to salt the pork—it's called "brine salt"—and took it out to the barn lot where the mules were hanging around. Both of them came right up to the fence. Ole Lou was the first one to check it out. But it didn't take her long to decide she didn't want any of it. She stuck her nose to it and put her nose as high into the air as she could and wiggled her upper lip, as mules and horses do when they smell an unpleasant odor. Little Liz couldn't take Ole Lou's action at face value, she had to smell of it, too. And she made the same ugly face as Ole Lou. It was a funny sight to a little boy to see both of them old mules standing there with their noses in the air trying to get a breath of fresh air.

Many times I have gone into the fields and my brother would be working the mules and I would throw rocks or dirt at them. Neither the mules nor my brother appreciated that. It was all he could do to prevent a run-a-way.

Jason Wilson lived across a huge field from us. Jason farmed on a much larger scale and more professional than my dad. He was also a sportsman. He did a lot of trapping in the winter. Jason and dad were good friends.

I guess I was about seven years old. Jason had been around or somehow I had become aware of his trapping activities and how he was scratching the hides on boards to dry for later sale. I was far too little and young to trap for raccoons or foxes.

It was in the dead of winter and we were out of school because of snow. I needed something to do. Thinking about Jason and what he was doing, I caught a mouse. I got a board large enough to dry a raccoon or fox hide, and I skinned the mouse. I couldn't get its hide on the large board, but I was in the smokehouse working on it and heard something. I looked around and there in the door stood Jason Wilson as big as life! He could not believe what he was seeing! He was looking for dad. Apparently he thought it was the funniest sight he had ever seen. He kidded me about it for months.

Mom kept a wash tub under the eve of the house to catch rain water for washing clothes and other purposes. Come spring, it was cat baptizing time. I would catch the cats and throw them into the tub of water. It didn't make them any better cats, just wet ones!

I was perhaps in the third grade at the Ono School, and I got into trouble—I kissed a little female classmate. Of course, she was angry. The teacher chewed me out over it and I promised to *never* do it again. So I waited a few days, and then I went up to the teacher's desk and on the pretext of asking a question and pretending to not understand her answer, I kept inching around to her side and when I got exactly in position, I kissed her! The whole classroom came unglued. I ran back to my seat and sat down. The poor teacher just sat there in stunned silence! There was not a word said about it—except the students all went home and told their parents. I didn't live that little prank down for years.

Not everything that I did mimicked older people, but a lot of it did. I do not know why I was given to menacing older people, perhaps it was because I spent nearly all of my time with my dad and my uncle. We kids of that era manufactured most of their entertainment. Several kids in the community were near my brother's age, and really none was my age. There were a few a couple of years' younger. That really put me at a disadvantage so far as friends were concerned. When I was very small, there was a Zimmerman family that lived nearby that had a little boy close to my age. I can just remember when they moved away. Then later on I developed a real close friendship with Eddie Stephens, the youngest child of Mr. and Mrs. Lester Stephens.

There was a period of time when I was in elementary school that I had a close friendship with Kenstill Eastham, the only child of Mr. and Mrs. Willard Eastham. I also enjoyed the friendship of Bruce Johnson, the youngest child of Mr. and Mrs. Otha Johnson; and Rudy Higginbotham, the only son of Mr. and Mrs. Raymond Higginbotham.

CHAPTER THREE

EARLY CHILDHOOD

When I was five years old, I started to school. It was in July 1949. I attended the Ono School—as it was known than and had been for many years. Its original name was Cedar Grove—named after a grove of cedar trees that was nearby. The first year that I attended, it was a two-room school. One room was used for grades first—fourth, and the other was for grades fifth—eighth. However, the next year the local school broad combined all eight grades in one room. From then on, it was a one-room school.

The Ono School was an old frame, white weather-boarded building with very high ceilings. It had three large windows on either side of the rooms. It was wired for electric service the first year I attended. It was heated by a coal stove which was situated in the middle of the room. The stove was vented with a six-inch oil-well casing. When the weather was very cold, we would move our desks out of their rows and place them as close to the stove as we could. Otherwise, the desks were in eight rows, one for each grade. It had a blackboard at the east end of the building behind the teacher's disk. It did not have a library, not even a dictionary.

The periods lasted for one hour. After it became a one-room school, the teacher had twelve and one-half minutes per grade to teach. The morning periods were given to Spelling, Reading,

English, and Arithmetic; then an hour's break for lunch and noon recess. In the afternoon, History and Geography were taught.

In my earliest school years, the school year began in July. We did not get a holiday until Thanksgiving and then only a half-day. Near Christmas, the older and bigger boys would be sent out to find and cut a Christmas tree and we always had a Christmas play. The last day of school prior to Christmas holidays, we would perform the play and the parents were invited to see it. In the early years, we only got a couple of days off for Christmas; however, a little later we got from a day or so before Christmas until a day or two after New Years' day.

Christmas was an enjoyable and exciting time— notwithstanding the fact that I received very little in the way of presents or gifts. Dad was not given to spending money for Christmas presents. Mom did the best she could and generally whatever my brother and I received, she got with money she earned from gathering walnuts, cracking them, and selling the kernels. She would set for days with an old pressing iron turned upside down between her knees and crack those walnuts with a claw hammer.

After the corn was harvested, the tobacco stripped and sold, the walnuts cracked and sold, and Christmas over, mom would piece quits and quit. She tried to complete one quit per year. Her quits were not fancy ones but of very high quality. She made them from scrap cloth cut in three to four inch pieces either squares or triangles. She did all of the sewing by hand.

Mom raised her own cotton. We were the only family in the community that grew our own cotton. It was a practice that mom brought with her from Wayne county. Her family had done the same thing for years, not only for padding their quits but to spin for thread to knit the family's socks. For years she, and to a lesser extent, I seeded the cotton by hand. A very slow process! Eventually, we were given a little hand-made cotton gin, and mom and I sat for hours on cold winter nights and ginned cotton. The gin was a simple construction. Just two small wooden rollers mounted on vertical pieces of wood that were nailed to a horizontal board which we placed between two chairs and sat on. The rollers had a handle on each one at opposite ends and one would turn one handle in one direction and the other one would turn the other handle in the opposite direction and feed the cotton in. As the cotton went through the gin, it pushed the seeds out and took the cotton on through to the other side.

Mom would "card" the cotton on a tool called cotton cards. They were made of two pieces of wood approximately 4 X 10 inches with a 6 inch or so handle and on one side of the wood pieces were studded with very short, stiff wire. She used these to clean the cotton and to make it very fine. The process made what is called "bats." She used the bats to pad her quits.

One eventful time in my young life was "hog killing day." Dad always raised two hogs for meat. He would buy two forty to fifty pound pigs in early summer and feed them until November or December and kill and butcher them.

The eventful day actually began a day or two before. Dad would first get a bunch of wood together to heat the water. Then he got up extra early on the morning of the butchering and filled two cast iron kettles with water and started the fire. Soon Uncle Addie would arrive and they would go to the hog lot and kill one of the hogs and bring it to the back yard on a slid. Then they would pour boiling water on it out of the kettles to loosen the hair and then scrape the hair off of the hog. Next they would hang it up by its rear legs and gut it, cut its head off; get down and dress it out. Then they would get the meat into the smokehouse and salt it to cure it.

That night after the cows were fed and milked, dad would bring a shoulder of meat in the house and he and mom would grind it into sausage. The next morning, mom would fry the sausage and put it into quart jars and can it for future use. While mom was taking care of the sausage, dad would be in the back yard rendering the lard. As he and Uncle Addie dressed the meat, they trimmed away the excessive fat. Dad had to cook the fat for four hours or longer to get the lard out and for it to keep without spoiling. The left over product, actually the skin of the pork, were cracklings. They were tasty. In fact the pork skins sold in stores today is a poor excuse for home-cooked cracklings.

By the time I reached ten to twelve years old, dad had become so cantankerous that I could not talk with him. Actually, I was not really close to my dad. I can honestly say that I never had a meaningful conversation with my dad in my life and neither did my brother. Both my brother and I were closer to Uncle Addie than we were to dad. We could talk with Uncle Addie but not dad.

My mother was truly a good woman. However, she was not the best of mothers. Her good qualities were her religious faith, her truthfulness, honesty, and devoted wife. She was easily persuaded. Once she was told something and she believed it, her opinion could not be altered. She had only a fourth grade education.

While I was a student at the Ono school, most of my teachers were unremarkable, as well as the time I spent there. The event when I kissed my little classmate and then my teacher were interesting. Another interesting event was when a little boy, Roger Brown, let the secret out that one of his teachers was not wearing any bloomers. That wasn't the teacher I kissed. I though that she was going to kill little Roger before school was out. For the remainder of the school term, he could do nothing correct. She made his life misable!

However, one teacher really stands out. He was Mr. Edwin Wisdom from Jamestown. Mr. Wisdom was an incredibly well educated man. Some who knew him well claimed that he got his education from correspondence courses and diploma mills. He was somewhat of a veterinarian, and doctor, too. He died not long ago. He was more than ninety years old. He is at rest in the Concord cemetery in Russell County. His grave marker reads: "Edwin 'Doc' Wisdom." He was a very smart man, and I fondly remember the days I spent under his instructions.

During the summer before Mr. Wisdom came to teach at

the Ono School, I had spent a week with Ray and Eskay. I had helped Ray work on his farm. Mr. Wisdom lived close to the farm and I had met him at that time. Ray and I didn't do much work, but he gave me a fishing rod and reel for what I did. Mr. Wisdom's wife was Elmer Eastham's daughter—the man that Ray's brother and another Esto Dunbar had killed—and Willard Eastham's sister.

Mr. Wisdom was truly one of my heroes. Mom didn't approve of our friendship. Mr. Wisdom was a Seventh Day Adventist and mom was concerned that he would have a negative influence upon me. He didn't.

During my preteen and teenage years, I was very fond of Ray and Eskay. Ray and I went fishing and hunting together a lot. They came over to church an average of twice a month and then on to our home. After lunch, often Ray and I would go fishing or hunting—depending on the weather and the season. Ray was a man I could talk to without a problem. Eskay didn't pay a lot of attention to me. I do not recall ever having a one-on-one conversation with her. She devoted her time to talking with mom, dad, and Uncle Addie. Ray and I got our fair share of gray squirrels and small pan fish.

Ray had a Winchester, Model 03, .22 Cal. rifle that I dearly loved to shoot. It was clearly the best shooting rifle I ever shot. Years later I brought a new Winchester, Model 190, but it was not a comparable gun to Ray's Model 03.

CHAPTER FOUR

TEENAGE YEARS

After being graduated from the Ono School, I went to the Russell County High School at Russell Springs.

I was the only eighth grade student from Ono to go on to high school that year. There were several other Ono students going to high school that had graduated a year or two before, but not that year. All of them were girls and there was not a single male student at the high school that I knew.

I hated high school with a passion. There were several reasons for my dislike of high school. One of the reasons was the fact that I didn't know any of the boys, and they all had friends from their respective schools. Other reasons were because I could not particulate in any extracurricular activities; could not attend any sporting events; could not take any courses that required extra expenses such as typing, or go on field trips. Dad's ideal of a kid getting an education was to go to school. Nothing else mattered—such as adequate supplies, personal friendships, sports, clubs, trips, etc.

When I was not in school, I was working. Before school, I helped feed and milk the cows; after school, I worked in the crops and helped feed and milk the cows plus other chores. None of the work was done by modern methods. We milked by hand. Most of the hay was hauled in lose, *i.e.*, not bailed, or was stacked in the field; the corn was harvested by hand and shoveled out of the wagon by hand. Our firewood for heating and cooking was cut by hand with a crosscut saw and split with an ax and hauled to the house. We finally got a chainsaw to cut wood.

I was making failing grades and dropped out of high school in my junior year.

A few months after leaving school, I enrolled in a correspondence automotive repair course offered by the American School of Chicago, Illinois. It took me about nine months to complete the course.

When I was sixteen years old, I made a profession of faith during a revival at the Square Oak church and was baptized in Goose Creek in the Fonthill community. At the age of seventeen, I brought my first Bible, which I still have, a new Scofield reference bible for $7.50 from Dewey Cooper, who was running a hardware store in Russell Springs at that time and later became a Baptist minister.

I devoted a lot of my spare time to studying the Bible. I attended church every Sunday, and listened to several preachers on radio. Nationally, they were—among others—Billy Graham and Garner Ted Armstrong; regionally, Byron Jessup and Walter Strong; locally, L. R. Hart and later Roger Popplewell.

The local Baptists liked Billy Graham, but despised Herbert W. and Garner Ted Armstrong. I didn't understand their resentment because I failed to find fault with their messages broadcasted on the radio, or their teachings in *The Plain Truth* magazine.

Later on, I, too found faults with some of their teachings, but still admired their in-dept analysis of the news and prophecy interpretations.

During my seventeenth year, 1961, I got my first car, a 1956 Buick. I had saved money from Social Security benefits that I received because of dad's age, at the rate of ten dollars per month. I gave four hundred and fifty dollars for the car. It was a very good car. I drove it for several years.

Right after my eighteenth birthday, I got a job as a mechanic at Black Motors in Russell Springs. I worked at Black's for about two years until I married and rented a farm.

While working at Black Motors, when I was eighteen, I met Byron Jessup. He was one of nine children of Rev. and Mrs. Walter Jessup of Gulfport, Mississippi. All seven of their boys were preachers. Charles was the oldest, whom I never met. However, I did have the opportunity to meet Jimmy and Walter, Jr. I never met either of the daughters. Walter, Sr., had been a traveling preacher and had founded several churches in Mississippi when he was a young man, following brush harbor revivals.

Before I met Byron, he and his brothers had held a huge revival in Louisville, Kentucky. They had rented a theater and packed it out night after night for weeks. Hundreds of people had been converted to Christ. A relatively short time after the close of the Louisville revival, Byron settled in Lexington, Kentucky, and founded and built Revival Tabernacle. For years it consisted of only the basement and roof, but for several years now it has been a completed beautiful building.

Some locals arranged for Byron to come to Jamestown and hold church services in the Circuit Courtroom in the Russell County Courthouse. My brother-in-law, Ray Chrisman really liked him and that is how I heard of him and started going to his services. Later on he held two or three tent revivals in Jamestown. I really liked Byron and maintained a close relationship with him for several years.

I never met Walter Strong. I listened to him a lot on radio and saw him a few times on T.V. He was a wonderful minister of the gospel.

During my teenage years, Rev. S. B. Rowe--who at that time was pastor of the First Baptist Church in Russell Springs, which was then located at the intersection of Wilson Street and Highway 127--and Leo Chrisman had a burning desire to build a church in the Flanagan community. Flanagan was the next community south of Ono. Leo taught school at the one-room Flanagan school for years. I have heard him say time and again, "where there is a school, there ought to be a church." Rev. Rowe and Mr. Chrisman eventually convinced the members of the Missionary Baptist congregation at Square Oak to help build a church at Flanagan. A local gentleman, Alonzo Holder donated land for the new church in a grove of pine trees that he owned. It was built and became the Lakeview Baptist Church. The beginning of the Lakeview church was the beginning of the end of the Missionary congregation at Square Oak. After some of the members left to go to Lakeview, only dad and mom, Alonzo Popplewell, and S. B. Coffey were left at Square Oak. They soon dissolved it and only the Separate Baptists were left at Square Oak as an organized congregation.

Rev. S. B. Rowe and Leo Chrisman put their hearts and souls into making Lakeview a success. Also Mace Flanagan and Ed Lee Crocket put a lot of money into it. They built a nice building. The local residents of Flanagan-- except for the families of Mace Flanagan, Ed Lee Crocket, and Alonzo Holder (Benard Hughes' family who went to another church in another community)--were unchurched.

At about the same time the building at Lakeview was being considered, an elderly couple from Lincoln County—John and Mary Carter—had built a vacation cottage on Lake Cumberland in the Indian Hills community on Tucker Ridge. The Carters had been attending the Clear Fork Baptist church at Eli. The Carters convinced the Clear Fork congregation to help build a church at Indian Hills. The new church became Indian Hills Baptist. A local young minister, Cleveland Johnson, became its pastor.

The Indian Hills church held its services on Sunday afternoons and several members of Clear Fork came to help with the services. Mrs. Jewell Zimmerman was one of the faithful Clear Fork members that came and taught Sunday school. She was one of the finest Christian ladies that I ever knew, and a wonderful Sunday school teacher. The Carters, Rev. Johnson, and the Clear Fork people, made Indian Hills a successful church.

On the other hand, Lakeview never did get to going well. The people of the Flanagan community—except those mentioned above—were mostly Polstons and had never gone to church and, in actuality, were almost all moon-shiners and bootleggers and had been all of their lives. They were a very difficult lot to get into church. In real terms, the Lakeview church was not a success, despite the best efforts of Rev. Rowe, Leo Chrisman, Mace Flanagan, Ed Lee Crocket, and Alonzo Holder. They tried. It was eventually closed.

A few years later but within this general same time frame, Alonzo Popplewell's wife, Roxie, became disillusioned with the Separate Baptists for some reason, and to their consternation, withdrew her membership. At this time, the Missionary Baptist congregation at Square Oak had been dissolved for several years. For one thing, she did not like the idea of the Separate Baptists having total control of the property where the church sat. Perhaps the Separate Baptists were discussing building a new building on the property. The property had been donated by Mark Wilson, Roxie's husband's uncle.

Roxie approached dad and mom and broached the subject of organizing a community church at Square Oak. They agreed. Alonzo and Roxie Popplewell, dad and mom, and I became the five charter members of the Ono Community Church.

The Separate Baptists eventually acquired property behind the Square Oak church and built a new building. A while after they got their new building finished, we moved the Square Oak building a couple of hundred yards west of its location and situated it on a corner at the crossroads where an old dilapidated store building had been on property donated by Alonzo and Roxie Popplewell. We completely remodeled it and put brick around it and made it into a nice, modern building.

However, before the remodeling was completed, I withdrew my membership. I left the church partly to protect it and partly because of some disagreements among some of the members. Roxie was chagrined at my leaving.

Looking back now forty years later, I somewhat regret getting involved with the community church project. Not because it failed to prosper. In fact, it did. Several residents of the community that had never been given to attending church were converted and became members of the new church, and it has continued to do very well. We got some really devoted ministers to come and serve as our pastors and helpers. Some of them were Dewey Cooper, Tobe Simpson and Walter Compton. In hindsight, I think everybody's efforts would have been better spent trying to serve the community rather than moving and remodeling a church. And I really do not have a problem with the Separate Baptists. I do not agree with them on every point of doctrine or belief, but they are very dedicated Christians.

During the time I was involved with the community church, the Carters from Indian Hills visited my parents and wanted me to come over to their church on Sunday afternoons. I was at work at the time of their visit and didn't meet them that day. However, I started going there on Sunday afternoons.

CHAPTER FIVE

YOUNG ADULTHOOD

I eventually met a young lady, LaVone Johnson, at the Indian Hills church. LaVone often led the singing and sang special songs and participated in others leadership parts of the services. She was by far the most active young person in the church. She lived with John and Julie Stephens. While I did not know her until I started going to church there, I learned that she was the daughter of Dora and her late mother Bessie (Sullivan) Johnson. Her mother had died when she was eighteen months' old, and John and Julie Stephens had taken her and reared her as their foster daughter. Everyone in the church viewed her as being a remarkable fine young lady.

Eventually, LaVone and I started dating and the people of the church were extremely pleased that we were dating and often spoke to me about her being a wonderful, fine Christian lady. My parents were very opposed to my dating her because of her dad's background. My parents had opposed everyone my older brother had dated; it didn't matter that their families were nice, respectable people.

I knew LaVone's dad but not real well. When I was a small kid, he and Kirby Eastham had come to our home and borrowed a little money from dad. I knew that he had once had his picture in the local paper and had been likened to the famous movie star, Gabby Hayes. The paper had found him to be an entertaining sort of character. I knew that he was an old time moon-shiner and drunk.

Even at that young age, I knew of fine young women whose dads had been drunks that had gone on to do very well in life. A couple of them were the daughters of Mace Flanagan, who had been a leader in building the Lakeview church. He had been a drunk before he became a Christian, and all of his children grow up to be as well respected as any in the community. I know of alcoholics that have had a child to grew up and become a minister of the gospel. I have known ministers whose kids became drunks. History proves that children cannot be judged by their parents' behavior, and parents cannot be judged by their children's behavior.

Later on LaVone revealed to me that John and Julie would not allow her dad to visit or have any contact with her when she was growing up. Her dad didn't have any close relatives in the area, and her mother's family didn't want her after her mother's death. In fact, her dad's family had nearly all died in a short period of time of tuberculosis (T.B.)--the same disease that had killed my dad's first wife—however, her mother had died of pneumonia.

John and Julie were tenant farmers for Mark Wilson, the same Mr. Wilson whom had donated the land for the Square Oak church many years earlier. Mr. Wilson was a wealthy man. He had never married and had lived with his brother, King, until King died and then he lived alone. They had large land holdings on Wolf Creek until it was taken by the federal government for the impounding of Lake Cumberland. He also had large land holdings above the creek on Tucker Ridge. During Mr. Wilson's illness and death, Julie and another tenant, Pete McBeath, had taken care of him. Mr. Wilson's estate sale was held the day LaVone and I were married in September 1964. Much of Mr. Wilson's real estate was later developed into a KOA Campground and Resort near Alligator Dock II on Lake Cumberland.

Mr. Wilson was a remarkable character. He never owned a tractor or automobile or had electric service in his home. In fact, the home where LaVone was reared did not have electric service. His farming methods were primitive even by today's Amish standards. It was reported by those whom knew him well that he nailed the covers down on his bed at night, ostensibly to prevent being robbed.

Years earlier while he and King were living on the creek, a robbery had been attempted at their home and King killed the robber. He was a local man, last name, Taylor, which lived a few miles away.

Mark and King's parents had died long ago and were buried on the creek. When the lake was coming in, the government relocated all of the graves that were known to exist to other locations. A large "government section," as they are known, is located on the back side of the Square Oak church cemetery. Mark had his parents' remains relocated to a corner of a field he owned at the edge of the Holt Cemetery on Tucker Ridge, and built a building over their graves. He and his brother, King, were also buried under the building. Mark left a trust fund to maintain the building.

Mr. Wilson was sort of a godfather to the residents of Tucker Ridge. Back in the forties and fifties the whole area was very economically depressed. Almost everybody either farmed or made moon-shine liquor. The farmers didn't get much for the products they raised and labor was cheap. In the earliest of Mark's life he had paid as little ten cents for a twelve-hour day's work. At the time he became too old to take care of his business and had to rent his land out to tenants, he was paying only three dollars per day. The people lived by raising large gardens and preserving their fruits and vegetables. They either lived in their homes—many of which were little more than shanties—or tenant houses. It didn't take much money for them to live.

One of Mark's most faithful employees was Junnie Oakes, whom Mark called "Ole Goat." Junnie could sit and reminiscence hilarious anecdotes for hours about his and Mark's bygone days. More than once in the fall they wouldn't have any work to do, so Junnie or one of the other employees would set Mark's woods on fire. As some would fight the fire, someone else would reset it behind them. They would keep the fires burning for a month just to earn a few dollars, or less, per day. More than once during a winter when Junnie needed a day or two of work, he would go into the woods and move boundary line markers—a rock—and go tell Mark that a neighbor was stealing his land. Mark would send Pete McBeath, one of his other tenants, to get Otha Whittle to come and re-survey the questionable location. This put a few dollars in Junnie's pocket and was no small harassment to Mark's neighbors, mainly DeSoto Popplewell. Otha Whittle didn't have a license of any kind. He worked under a "grandfather clause" because he had been surveying land, preparing deeds and Wills since before licenses were required. When he died, that practice came to an end. Nobody else will ever be able to do what he did without a license.

In addition to Junnie Oakes, some of Mark's other employees were brothers John and Oscar Tucker, Newt Smith, and John and Julie Stephens. Mark would give LaVone a few days' work so she could get new clothes for school when she was a little girl.

Mark had an old mule to die. First, Junnie solicited the job of burning him. That didn't work. After days trying to burn him, Junnie persuaded Mark that he should bury him. Junnie worked for days digging a grave. By the time Junnie got the old mule to his final resting place, he was about rotten.

LaVone and I were married at the Indian Hill's church. The families of Barnard Highfield and Floyd Hester, owners of Highfield and Hester Flooring, of Louisville, had a vacation cottage on the lake, and were very fond of LaVone. When they were at the lake, they attended the services at Indian Hill and provided substantial support of the church. They insisted on paying for us having a church wedding.

After we were married, we rented a farm in the Eli community. I had a few cows and soon bought a few more, and we worked for other farmers in their tobacco and hay, etc. I also bought a few more pigs and raised them to become breeding stock. Before long I had feeder pigs to sell. Everything was going well for us.

In the spring of 1965, I bought a new Massy-Ferguson 135 tractor with plow, disk, mower, and cultivator for thirty-three hundred dollars. I borrowed the money from the Farmers Home Administration and the payments were something like five hundred dollars per year.

In October 1965, our first daughter, Bernice, was born. She was born at the Adair County Hospital in Columbia, Kentucky, and the total cost of the hospital bill was fifty dollars and fifty cents.

We stayed on the Eli farm until the spring of 1966. My Uncle Addie and Aunt Ollie decided to sell their farm, and a deal was made with dad to buy the farm on the condition that I get the place. LaVone and I moved to the place and continued to grow the tobacco crop on the rented farm at Eli for that year. This series of events were the beginning of mistakes that have followed and haunted me for the rest of my life.

When Eskay found out about the land deal that Uncle Addie and dad had made, she was extremely angry. She had a nasty confrontation with dad about it and his health deteriorated from that time forward. He was deeply troubled by Eskay's behavior.

Within a matter of days or a week or two, dad decided to make a Will. He had never considered making a Will before; however, given Eskay's behavior, he decided it would be in his other children's best interest. He left Eskay his interest in three pieces of real estate that he and Ray owned in Jamestown.

The Jamestown properties is a story in and of itself. An old doctor, Dr. Lawrence, had died and some of his property was up for sale. One was his old office building. It was an old, huge two-story building that he had used for his office, and reportedly he kept seriously ill patents there at times. It had a totally dark room in it where he finished X-rays. Next door was another huge two-story house that he had used for his residence--prior to his building the "Amaranth" mansion south of Jamestown on Highway 127. And next door to it was small residential type house. Ray and dad had bought all three buildings and properties for ten thousand dollars.

On the day of the sale, Ray came over to our home and picked him up to go to the sale. Uncle Addie had gone with them, too. After the sale, dad didn't say a word to mom about what they had done. A few days later Uncle Addie came over and mentioned it, not aware that dad had not told mom anything about it. Mom was irate! Dad had loaned Ray the money too pay for his share and it had taken almost all of dad's money to pay for all the property. They immediately started trying to sell the property. The small house sold fairly soon at a fair price. They tried to rent the building but largely to no avail. They were so big nobody wanted them—at any price.

In 1967, our second daughter, Julene, was born at the Adair County Hospital. By now I was deeply involved in church activities at the Ono Community and to a lesser degree at Indian Hills. It was around this time that I served as the Adult Bible Class Sunday school teacher at the Ono Community Church. I was twenty-three years old. I had engaged in a few revival services and had a weekly radio program on a station in Monticello, Kentucky. Also, by now Dad was totally disabled and I farmed the Addie farm and the home farm, too.

During our first or second summer on the farm, Bro. Cleveland Johnson decided that he wanted the Indian Hill church to find another pastor. Several of the members ask me if I would take the position. I really did not want to do it, but agreed to in order to be of service to the church and the community. A few days later, Rev. O'Neal Wade came to our home and told me that some of the members believed it would be better to have a member of the Baptist faith take the job and that I might cause a division within the church. He was going to take the position and be the church's pastor. The allegation that I might cause a division in the church really offended me, otherwise I was glad that he would do it; I told him okay; that was fine with me. I really did not want to do it anyway. It really did offend LaVone. It was her one and only home church and she had done a lot to support it by accepting leadership roles and playing music, etc. She dearly loved that church and the people that attended it.

Several members were very upset when they found out what Rev. Wade and a few other members had done. Some threatened to leave the church. I advised them that I wished they wouldn't do that. The church was small and weak anyway.

It wasn't long, only a few weeks, until rumors and gossip were traveling far and wide that Rev. Wade and one of the member's wife were engaged in an excessively friendly relationship. It wasn't long until it was not rumors and gossip. Dora Bowling and his wife got a divorce and Dora Bowling never lived another happy day for the remainder of his life. Dora Bowling was several years older than his wife. They had, as I recall, four children. At the time of their divorce, their children ranged in ages from approximately four to twelve.

The Indian Hill church soon closed and remained closed until Bro. Cleveland Johnson came back and reopened it. Later on I again attended services at the church. Several years later, I was at the church and some of the Bowling children had grown up and married and they were there singing. They were very talented singers and I enjoyed the service.

Rev. Wade served as pastor for another Baptist church for a year or longer and then became a Chaplin for the Kentucky National Guard.

In the meantime, Ray and dad had sold the Jamestown properties. In February 1969 Ray died. He and Eskay were at dads on Sunday and he seemed to be fine. Then or Tuesday, Jason Wilson stopped by and told mom and dad that he was in the hospital at Glasgow, Kentucky, and only had hours or a day or two at best to live. He was soon dead and his funeral was on Saturday. Then on March 6th dad passed away.

Eskay didn't know anything about dad's Will until after his death. Again, she was extremely angry! She was mad at everybody, my brother, my mom, her brother, and me. None of us had anything to do with it, dad made his own decisions and nobody told him what to do. He would come nearer listening to his brother Addie than anyone. Uncle Addie had some input into how he made his Will. She was all the more upset because the Jamestown property which was bequeathed to her had been sold. The home place had been left to mom for her life time and then to my brother, four thousand dollars left to my half-brother Carson, and the Addie farm to me.

My brother was appointed administrator as per the Will. Eskay finally agreed to accept four thousand dollars, the same as her brother was left. But the damage had been done. Her anger and unconscionable behavior had profited her nothing.

Dad was well aware of the situation with his Will after the Jamestown properties were sold. He was still upset with Eskay for raising an argument with him and knew that she would be unhappy with the matter. He considered changing his Will, but just left word that she should get four thousand dollars like Carson.

Carson didn't have much to say about it. He knew dad as well as anybody. He had basically had to leave home when he was sixteen years old because dad was working him to death for nothing. Carson knew that nobody could tell dad what to do and whatever he had done was of his own accord. However, after the settlement of the estate, I never saw Carson again. During his final illness, I was told by his wife's family that he was very ill. I was not notified when he passed away.

The last time I saw my niece, Mary Magdalene, was either at my dad's funeral or on Christmas day 1968. She had married Norris Russell of the Salem community when she was quite young. Norris was in the Air Force until he retired and then worked for charter air services. They lived in Mechanicsburg, Pennsylvania. They had one son, Scott. With the last few years, Magdalene "Maggie" and Norris relocated to the Salem community—where they were reared—in Russell County. Norris passed away on October 16, 2007 at the age of 76.

Carson had married Miss Rexroad when he was young and from his inherence from his mother's parents' estate he purchased a little farm in the Salem community. Carson and Ada live there until their daughter, Mary Magdalene, graduated from high school. Mary Magdalene wanted to go to college at the University of Kentucky at Lexington. They sold the little farm and relocated in Lexington. Mary ended up getting married rather than going to school. They purchased an apartment building and stayed in Lexington until Carson passed away. After Carson passed away, I think Ada lived with her daughter in Pennsylvania until her death. Carson and Ada are buried in the Salem Cemetery near the Salem Baptist Church.

When LaVone and I moved to my Uncle Addie's farm, we had a lot of work to do. Uncle Addie had been nearly blind for several years and nothing had been done on the farm. The fencing was a poor state of repair. I had to fence some of it before I could move my cows and hogs. It was crop preparing and near planting time so we worked nearly day and night for several weeks. We had a good crop year and all was well.

When winter came on, I started to lose cows. They die one after the other until they all were nearly gone. I never knew what happened to him. I do know from very reliable sources that Ray's car was seen on the road late at night. The next spring, my hogs got sick and I lost a lot of pigs. Again, I do not know what happened.

Also, after we moved to the farm, LaVone's dad, Dora Johnson lived nearby on a farm and it wasn't long until he began causing us a lot of problems. He was a troublemaking that enjoyed instigating anger amongst the neighbors by spreading rumors, gossip, innuendo, half-truths, and outright lies. What he did cost us a lot of money, property, and character. His behavior eventually caused LaVone to become an alcoholic. I handled the situation as long as I could—not the best I could, in hind sight—but fifteen years later LaVone and I were divorced. Her dad and his behavior are due all of the credit.

After it was too late, I realized that LaVone's dad hated her. Why? I do not know. He hadn't been with her any while she was growing up. He had lost two brothers in World War II and drawn twenty thousand dollars in benefits from the government and wasted it all. He bought a fine farm, rented it to a family, and then argued and complained about everything the man did until he just let the crops go and neither of them made anything that year. He sold the farm and drunk the money away. He had bought LaVone one eight dollar coat and nothing else during her childhood. The damage he did can never be undone and the cost never recovered.

I could criticize a lot of other people and say a lot of negative things, but it would achieve nothing good. What is done, is done. Nothing can change the past. History is as if it were carved in stone. I haven't derived any pleasure from recalling these events of the past. It is better to leave much unsaid. However, I do not believe it is wrong to tell the truth.

CHAPTER SIX

TROUBLESOME TIMES

Following the losses that we had suffered, the lose of the cows and hogs alluded to in the previous chapter, the next year LaVone and I decided to sell the farm and build an automotive repair shop in the Eli community. I built a nice building about thirty by forty-four feet. We had a good business and did well. I had an excellent mechanic helping me. But in the fall after working for me for about six months, he and his wife decided to go back to Denver. His wife was from out that way and he had worked in the area before, notwithstanding the fact he had been reared on Tucker Ridge.

LaVone had a brother and a half-brother in Indianapolis, Indiana, and she wanted to relocate there, partly because her dad was still causing problems for us. Her brothers painted a very rosy picture for us about how life was in Indiana. We sold the garage and relocated there. Our expectations in Indiana did not pan out, and, again, we suffered huge losses.

After more difficult and troubling times and drifting about, we ended up back in Kentucky, and in 1972 our son, Jackie Lynn, was born in Lexington, Kentucky. I continued to work in the automotive repair business, and for some periods of time in construction.

A few years later I decided to go back to school. I earned my GED and enrolled in Somerset Community College at

Somerset, Kentucky, and was graduated from it in 1978. I went on to Eastern Kentucky University at Richmond, Kentucky, for two years, leaving lacking nine credit hours of having earned a B.A. degree. At Somerset I majored in journalism, and at Eastern in political science.

When I left Eastern Kentucky University, I went to Dallas, Texas, seeking a job. I had a friend there that wanted me and my family to relocate to that area. I left around four o'clock in the morning and before night fall rumors were throughout the community that a neighbor's wife had gone with me.

I hardly knew the lady. I knew her brothers and father and her husband well. And her husband and her were having martial problems. They had a small child or maybe two.

I knew nothing of the matter until I called home late that night. LaVone told me the whole story. The lady and her child or children had visited LaVone that very afternoon. Her husband had heard the allegations and came and asked LaVone about it and she told him that she didn't know where his wife was at the moment, but she knew that she was not on the road to Texas with me because she had visited with her all afternoon.

The next afternoon the allegation was alluded to at a local country store and one of the customers said that he knew the story was a lie because I had left around four o'clock in the morning and he has seen the lady drive past his home at around ten o'clock.

I was in Texas for about a month and found that the same employment opportunity was available in Louisville, Kentucky, as there and came back home. I made a couple of inquires and found that there were people that still believed the outrageous allegation. Several years later people were still believing it.

LaVone and I both knew exactly where the allegations originated from—her dad. And every word of it was an outright lie.

The truth of the matter is, I never had a conversation with the lady. I was not acquainted with her. I knew her when I saw her, but beyond that I didn't really know her. And she absolutely never went anywhere with me at anytime!

I went to Louisville and had an opportunity to get a real good, high paying job with National Life of Vermont. They had to obtain a consumer report and got one from Equifax, the huge credit reporting agency in Atlanta, Georgia. It came back with the allegations that I had gone to Texas with "another woman." That false allegation cost me that job and thousands of dollars in earnings. I knew that whoever had provided the information knew me, but not well. At that time, I could not determine the source of the information.

After a period of time and some investigation, I discovered that Equifax had been Retail Credit and the Federal Trade Commission had taken it to court and had compiled a quarter of a million pages of documents and records from Retail Credit and had forced it to change its name. I also discovered that Equifax had contacts with Farm Bureau to provide background information for the reports.

It did not take me long to figure out that Robert Porter, Farm Bureau's agent in Russell Springs, Kentucky, was the source of the negative information to Equifax and his primary source was LaVone's dad. My loss amounted to tens of thousands of dollars.

Later I went to work in Louisville, Kentucky, as a paralegal for one of the best known but unpopular attorneys in Kentucky, Dan T. Taylor III. Dan specialized in civil rights and criminal law. At the time I worked for him, he had one hundred and fourteen murder cases behind him. He had been practicing law for forty years and had been held in contempt of court numerous times and had his bar license suspended at least once. His disbarment case had been heard by the United States Supreme Court. His problems with the Kentucky Bar Association are well documented in Kentucky's Court Reporters.

After I left the employ of Dan Taylor, I became an insurance agent and worked at that business for the next five years.

Then I became a trucker in 1987 and have been employed in that business since then.

After LaVone and I were divorced, I didn't date anyone for years. I tried to take care of our children.

As I said in the *Preface*, this is not a "tell-all" book. Although I have aired some dirty laundry, far more have been left untold than have been revealed. There are several reasons for this fact. One, I am not going to make excuses for my mistakes and misdeeds; and secondly, I am not going to point to others' guilt. I have simply forgiven the wrongs of the past and I am trying to move forward with my life. My life's experiences have left me suffering from two maladies: Post Traumatic Stress Disorder and situation depression.

As I bring this chapter to a close, I do not consider myself to be of major importance. What is important is my faith, which in many ways has been a failure, too. What I have done, is my doing and I take full responsibility for my actions.

God has been incredibly good to me. I have never experienced a serious illness and my health is very good. But even more important than anything else, God has given me a vast knowledge of His word. And with time, the forces of evil do not change. God's men of high calling have also always experienced hardships and prosecutions. Not a word in God's Holy Word ever suggested that any change would be forthcoming. His Word says exactly the opposite. There is not a doubt in my mind, my hardships were a result of my faith, and the fact that I would not allow anybody to control what I believed or my positions on matters of faith.

My experiences are not entirely unique. I know of one fine minister of the gospel that was ruined on what I believe were lies. I know of another one that was lied about, but they never got legs and went anywhere. I know of another one that some people tried to destroy but were unsuccessful.

CHAPTER SEVEN

FAREWELL

As I look back on my life, I have made many, many mistakes. So much of what I have done could have been done differently and much better. I have tried to make the best decisions that I could given the circumstances that I had to deal with. I have remained silent about a lot of matters and issues.

I could level a lot of charges and accusations against a lot of people and blame them for my shortcomings and failures. But that would profit nothing. Many times bad things are better left unsaid.

Everybody has done things that they shouldn't have done. That's human. And everybody has a duty to forgive.

The day will surely come when we all shall stand before our Creator and be judged by His righteousness. That will be a day of justice for all, including me.

I have cut life's story short on details because my life and I am not important except for my faith in God. I have certainly cut the criticism of other people short, too. The limited amount of criticism I have engaged in has been done for the purpose of teaching others to not follow in their footsteps, but to learn from their mistakes and misdeeds.

I have taken several steps to change the course of my life. One, about twenty years ago, I left Russell County and relocated approximately thirty miles away in Pulaski County and have resided there ever since. That was a good and positive thing.

After leaving Russell County, I did not attend church for almost fifteen years. During that time, I listened to gospel radio a lot and occasionally attended a truck-stop chapel service.

After working for several different trucking companies, I worked for two or three years for Garner Transportation in Somerset and made an average of two and half trips a month to the West Coast—Southern or Northern California, Oregon or Washington. Late one night on a cross-country trip in Missouri or Kansas, I heard a minister on the radio. I don't recall his name or where he was from except he was from somewhere in Indiana. He had been somewhere in a minister's study or to a conference and saw a book entitled *It's Never too Late for a New Beginning*. He based his message that night on the title of that book and the parable of the prodigal son and the Pharisee (Luke 15:11−32). Some of the high points of his message were that when the prodigal son came to himself, he realized that it was not too late for him to have a brand new beginning; about how happy the father was that his wayward son had returned; he talked a lot about the older brother, the Pharisee, the greed and jealousness in his heart and that he was angry because he wanted to do what his younger brother had done; and that sin was in his heart. It was one of the top ten best messages I have ever heard. I thought about it for weeks and, in fact, still do.

In the meantime, LaVone remarried and her new husband was killed in an automobile accident. All of our children are grown and doing okay. Bernice earned a B.A. degree from Lindsey Wilson College at Columbia, Kentucky; Julene earned a Master's degree at the same school; and Jackie Lynn has been seriously injured in a couple of accidents.

LaVone's dad, Dora Johnson, laid drunk and his legs were frostbitten and had to be amputated and he died in a nursing home. Tucker Ridge is a much more peaceful place to live. I was not the only victim of his rumors and gossip, which have now ceased.

In 1993, my half-sister died and left her estate, valued at approximately three hundred and fifty thousand dollars, to her niece, Mary "Maggie" Magdalene Russell. However, no mention is made of "Maggie" or any other relatives in her obituary as published in *The Times Journal* of Russell Springs. It reads: "Eskay Chrisman, age 81, of Jamestwon (*sic*) died Tuesday, March 30, 1993, at the Russell County Hospital.

"She was born October 8, 1911, in Pulaski County, to the late Luettia Wilson Anderson and M.S. Anderson.

"She was preceded in death by her husband, Edward Ray Chrisman.

"Mrs. Chrisman was a member of the Square Oak Separate Baptist Church.

"Funeral services were Thursday, April 1, 1993, at 10 a.m., at Bernard Funeral Home Chapel, with Rev. Donnie Coffey and Rev. Garfield Gosser officiating.

"Pallbearers were Clifford Wilson, Billy Johnson, Lee Smith, Miles McGowan, Jimmy Dick and Bruce Lawless.

"Interment was in the Mill Springs National Cemetery in Nancy."

Her brother's obituary reads vastly different: "Carson Anderson, age 74, of Lexington, formerly of Russell County, passed away Sunday, January 24, 1982, at the Good Samaritan Hospital.

"Mr. Anderson was a member of the Lexington Calvary Baptist Church and the Russell Springs Masonic Lodge #941.

"He was a son of the late M. S. Anderson and Sarah Luettia Wilson Anderson.

"Survivors include his wife, Eva Ada Rexroad Anderson, Lexington; one daughter, Mrs. Mary M. Russell, Mechanicsburg, Pennsylvania; one grandchild; two half-brothers, Orvis Anderson, Russell Springs, and Artis Anderson; one sister, Mrs. Eskay Chrisman, Jamestown.

"Funeral services were Wednesday, January 27, 1982, at ten o'clock AM at the Bernard Funeral Home Chapel, with Bro. Morris Gaskins officiating.

"Pallbearers were Vic Rexroad, Mike Rexroad, Paul Luttrell, Paul Whittle, Morris Whittle, and Mitchell Whittle.

"Burial was in the Salem Cemetery.

"Masonic Rites were held Tuesday night, January 26, 1982, at 7:30 P.M. by the Russell Springs Lodge."

In 1990, a friend introduced me to Phyllis Brasher. Phyllis was a beautiful lady about nine months older than me. She had three sons by a previous marriage and their dad was deceased. She was from a fine family in Leslie County around Hyden, Kentucky, but had lived in Somerset for several years. She had a sister in Florida and another in Virginia; and a brother in Dayton, Ohio, and one remained in the Hyden area. After her husband died, she had married Leroy McMullin of Somerset but that marriage lasted only a few months. Leroy was an admitted alcoholic, but otherwise a really nice guy.

When we first met, she started telling me horror stories about how Leroy had abused her. She won my heart and sympathy. She claimed that she was so traumatized by Leroy's abuse that she was fearful of staying alone and had kept her youngest son, Jeffrey, with her. At that time he was about twenty-eight years old. He was a drunk and dope user.

We soon started to discuss marriage. She started pressuring Jeffrey to get a job and move out on his own. I am still inclined to believe that she was serious at that time. However, Jeffrey kept finding excuses to not seek work.

I got Phyllis a fairly nice little engagement ring. She would refuse to set a wedding date, and Jeffrey was making no effort to get a job and get out on his own, so I finally told her I wanted the ring back. I knew that she dearly loved that ring and would refuse, which she did. So one day, just joking, I told her I would sue her to recover the ring. She dared me to do it. I told her I would and I did! I asked the court to force her to give the ring back or get married.

Bill Estep, the local reporter for *The Lexington Herald-Leader* of Lexington picked up on the case and called me for an interview. He ran an article about it and the Associated Press wire services picked it up and ran it nation or maybe worldwide. Phyllis' sisters in Florida and Virginia saw the stories and called her wanting to know what in the world was going on.

A media representative for the Diana Sawyer television show called me and wanted to arrange a T.V. appearance. He told me that a lawyer in Chicago had filed a similar action and they wanted to arrange for both couples to be in New York at the same time. I told him to send Phyllis a letter. He did—overnight--via FedEx! She didn't bite. To state it extremely mildly, she was angry!

A local attorney, D. Bruce Orwin, took her case *pro bono*—that is, without a fee or for free. He wasted a lot of his valuable time, but couldn't get it a final deposal. The case was in court for months. Finally, she decided that we would be married. We were in Monticello, Kentucky, on the first day of September, 1992.

When we at the wedding, and the County Judge-Executive was getting ready, I was thinking that this was going to be the most famous wedding he had ever done, he just didn't know it at that time. Indeed it was! Within days, Bill Estep had it back in *The Lexington Herald-Leader* again. The time we were together, I never again saw her as angry as she was at Bill Estep!

We finally were divorced in 1994. She advanced a lot of reasons and excuses for wanting a divorce, but truth was she could not face up to the lies she had told me.

When we got into divorce court she started lying on me. That got my attention. I began a full scale investigation. I examined her and Leroy's divorce file and found that she had made serious allegations concerning abuse. She claimed that he had broken her nose and put her in the hospital. Leroy's attorney, Bruce Singleton, a top rated Somerset counselor, was very concerned that Leroy was in big trouble. If Leroy had known her friends and background as I came to know them and had furnished that information to Mr. Singleton, Phyllis and her lawyer would have been in big trouble. She was trying to fraudulently obtain property from Leroy and, in fact, succeeded.

I knew a family that was very dear friends of hers and I knew that they would not lie. They were a very dedicated church going family. I knew that they had been the best of friends when she was married to Leroy. So I arranged to take the gentleman's deposition. His deposition proved that they were the best of friends at the time of her marriage to Leroy; that she was in and out of their home on a daily bases at that time; he had no knowledge of her ever having a broken nose, or of ever being hospitalized. I also arranged to take Leroy's deposition and the high points of it were that he had never injured her; Jeffrey had drank his beer and wouldn't get a job or work, and that she would lie.

When she was ready to file for divorce, she went to her home town of Hyden. A few days after filing the action, she came back to Somerset. Since neither of us was a resident of Leslie county, I filed a motion to dismiss it and it was granted by the court. Then she filed a new action in Somerset, and I once again filed a motion to dismiss on the grounds of *res judicia*—that is, a like action had been filed in another court and disposed of. We were in court for months, much to the displeasure of her and her attorney and high entertainment for the members of the Pulaski county bar.

Circuit Judge William Cain finally granted her the divorce, and I sued him in federal court at London. Federal Judge Coffman dismissed my case but remarked in her Opinion that he had granted the divorce illegally, but had jurisdiction over the case, and that dismissing my case against him was a "close call." Her Opinion was no laughing matter for Judge Cain. Not many months later he resigned his judgeship.

Kentucky's Constitution prohibits an appeal of a divorce case to Kentucky's higher courts. Therefore, the only appeal available to me was a petition to the United States Supreme Court. I seriously considered filing such a petition.

However, I considered the facts that she had repeatedly lied to me; lied about me; lied about Leroy; the cost involved, and that regardless of what I cared about her was irrelevant because she didn't care about me.

When I met Phyllis, I had not been going to church for a long time. It was continually on my mind and I desired to get back in attendance. I realized early on that Phyllis had extraordinary talents and abilities. It was absolutely amassing to see her ability to win the love of children. Every child that knew her had unconditional love for her. I realized that if I could get her to go to church, she could be an unequaled Sunday school teacher for small children.

She had been taken to church when she was a child, and as teenagers her sisters and she had formed a gospel singing group. Her brother, John Brock, in Hyden was a very dedicated Christian; both of her sisters were very dedicated Christians at their respective churches in Florida and Virginia, and her brother, William Brock, in Ohio, were one of the finest gentlemen that I have ever known.

I tried to save the marriage. And I could have forgiven her for everything. I understand that people are not perfect. Everybody has faults of some kind, and people make mistakes. I didn't ever hate her and still don't. I don't do anything to her for the purpose of harm. All I ever wanted was her to do what was right. Some in the medical profession believed that she was manic depressive also known as bipolar.

I have often wondered if I did her wrong. I honestly do not think I did. Actually as far as doing her real harm, I know I did not. Did I do anything that I should not have done? I probably did. If I could do everything over, I would do a lot of things different. For one, I would not have tried to hold on the relationship, and there certainly would not have been a marriage.

About a year after the divorce was final, she sent me a message via a friend that she would like for us to get back together. I considered the proposition for a few days, and sent her a message back that she had told me the last lie that she ever would. And that is the way it has been.

About ten years later when my daughter, Julene, was working toward her master's degree at Lindsey Wilson, one of her professors used the history of our divorce case for some of his comments in his class. Julene was astounded. After the class, she told him that one of the parties to the case was her dad. He was very surprised! Of course, all he knew about the matter were from media reports.

Numerous friends and acquaintances have asked me questions about Phyllis and the marriage and didn't understand why I fought to hold on to it like I did. The truth of the matter is I was fighting for her soul.

I have been going back to church for about five years. When I started back going to church, I went to Somerset Baptist Temple. Dr. S. David Carr founded that church several years ago. Then he built W.T.H.L. Christian radio station. For a long time, the station operated at low power, but now its programs are available worldwide via the internet at (Kingofkingsradio. com). I had listened to the radio station for ten years before I ever went to the church. Dr. Carr is absolutely one of the finest men of God that I have ever known. He is devoted to opposing alcohol, gambling, abortion, and other sinful behavior. He fights for and supports the Ten Commandments.

It is fairly easy to locate Bible believing churches. It is far more difficult to locate Bible *practicing* churches. The Somerset Baptist Temple is one of only a few churches that I am aware of that I would classify as being Bible *believing* and *practicing* churches. Another one is Revival Tabernacle in Lexington, Kentucky. Love Divine Baptist Church in Somerset, Kentucky, is a wonderful church. I'm confident that there are many others, I just not aware of their locations.

I considered writing a chapter on marriage, but decided to only write a segment on it. There are many different kinds of marriages. There good ones, bad ones, civil ones, religious ones, legal ones and illegal ones to name a few. Some are according to the will of God and some are not.

Marriage is defined in many different ways. In America and the West, marriage if generally thought of a man and a woman who have dated for a period of time and have fallen in love. The laws of most states, if not all, define marriage as a "civil contract." With marriage come certain responsibilities and obligations.

In 1995, Stephanie Coontz 1 wrote a remarkable book on the history of marriage

Marriage as defined in America and the West today is a fairly new innovation. Dating, obtaining a license from the state, and making the union a public record is actually only about four hundred years old.

For example, for a thousand years the Catholic Church accepted the marriage of a couple if they had agreed to marry. Coontz says it didn't matter if the agreement was made "in the kitchen or out by the haystack, they were in fact married." (p. 2)

In some parts of New Guinea men and women do not eat together because to do so is considered marriage.

In early Rome, no marriage license was required and there was no recognized distinction between cohabitation and marriage. The laws and customs of early Rome are very important because it was under these laws and customs that Christ was born into the world.

The state had no meaningful role in marriage until Byzantine Christian emperor Justinian (527–565) tried to make marriage dependent upon a state issued license.

Divorce in Rome was far more tightly regulated than marriage. During the reign of Augustus (27 B.C.–14 B.C.) divorce went from only notifying the other party to requiring seven witnesses. It was four more centuries (AD 449) before divorce required a statement of repudiation of the union. *Coontz*, p.80

Later Mohammed took a nine year old girl, Ayisha, to be his wife when he was fifty-three years old. In our modern times, he has been greatly condemned for this deed and adjudged to be a pedophile. However, the fact of the matter is, this sort of activity was not at all uncommon at that time. It was not uncommon for girls as young as two to three years old to be married. *Coontz*, p. 27 In many jurisdictions of the United States in the nineteenth century the age of consent for girls was from ten to twelve and in Delaware it was seven. *Coontz*, p. 127

For many hundred of years financial means was more of the controlling factor in who married whom than love. In many instances, a wife was chosen for a young man by the parents and the father of the wife paid a dowry to her husband.

49

I recall hearing my dad talk about Mr. Wilson giving Luettia a dowry when they married.

Under the teachings of Christ, marriage was to based on love, devotion, commitment, etc. And divorce was to be based upon unfaithfulness. When one partner to the union is unfaithful to the other by failing to do what the word of God commands them to do it is unfaithfulness and constitutes adultery and is grounds for divorce. Viewed in this context, the writings of the great prophet Jeremiah make perfect sense when he condemned Judah for having "committed adultery with stones and with stocks." (Jer. 3:9)

God's commandments for marriage are rather simple: "Husbands loves your wives, even as Christ also loved the church and gave himself for it." (Eph. 5:25) And wives are to honor and obey their husbands. "Let your women keep silent in the churches: for it is not permitted unto them to speak; but they are commanded to be under obedience, as also saith the law." (I Cor. 14:34)

Christ came to this world in obedience to his Father, God. Obedience per the law indicates a hierarchy of authority. At the top is God, then the son, Christ, then man, and lastly women. Men have a very serious obligation to love and honor their wives.

This writings of Apostle Paul have been much discussed in Sunday school classes. It clearly does not mean that women have no place in the church. The sixteenth chapter of Romans clearly shows that Paul had a lot of help from women and he mentioned them individually by name and expressed great appreciation for what they had done to help him advance the gospel.

God has used women for his honor and glory for a very long time. For example, God used Deborah for a judge of Israel and Israel "prevailed against Jabin." (Jud. 4:4 and 24); and God made Esther a queen (Esth. 2:17); and Christ used Mary Magdalene, Joanna, and Mary, the mother of James, and the other women with them to notify the apostles that he had risen (Luke 24:10).

It is not the women church workers that constitute the problems with our society and culture today. The liberal women and ungodly men are at the root of our problems.

I believe that there is no rational or logical way to view America--and to a lesser extent the West in general--except that America is Christ's church-state. It has only recently come to my attention that the late Dr. Jerry Falwell shared this view. It is the land given to a people to take his gospel to the world in the later days of the church-age.

History can be a good teacher. History teaches that the world has not been given to righteousness. Most of the generations of the world have been very evil. Therefore, our best instructions come from the Bible. I believe that the Bible clearly teaches that there are obligations and responsibilities dictated to both parties of a marriage and if either fails or refuses to honor his or her obligations and responsibilities that divorce is acceptable according to the scriptures.

PART TWO
MY FAITH

CHAPTER EIGHT

GOD AND MAN'S RELATIONSHIP

I

Introduction

At a time when the gospel is broadcast and telecasted around the world twenty-four hours a day seven days a week, it would seem that nobody should have a lack of the knowledge of God. However, there is a phenomenal lack of knowledge and understanding of God and His relationship with mankind.

There are many reasons for this phenomenal lack of knowledge. One of the reasons are the fact that the gospel is foolishness to the unbelievers (I Cor. 1:18). Other reasons include the negative stigma perpetrated against Christianity by the mass media and echoed by the American Civil Liberties Union (ACLU) along with anti-God litigants and liberal judges who think that they are smarter than God; the eviction of God from our public schools and public square; too much preaching and teaching in our churches and via the mass media in a format too advanced to be understood by the unchurched; and the churches having failed in the execution of their commission.

Another deeply troubling phenomenon is the fact that unchurched people are given to developing a "religion" of their own invention. This ignorant theology is not limited to America or the West. It is a repeated practice dating from the beginning of time. The first individual to engage in this sort of behavior was Adam and Eve's son, Cain. The practice has never ended.

II

Early Times

There is a fundamental relationship between God and man. God created man and created a relationship with him at that time. This relationship is both simple and complex. It is simple because it is easy to understand in its most fundamental sense, and, on the other hand, too difficult to understand.

"In the beginning, God created. . ." (Gen. 1:1) says the Holy Bible. The world was without form and void (Gen. 1:2). Herein may lay the cause for scientists' confusion which gave rise for the theory of evolution. It is undeniable that there have been changes in the world since its creation. For example, there is no doubt that the earth—lands portion of the world—consisted of one continent at its creation. There are three reasons for this belief: One, the Bible says that in the days of Peleg "the earth divided." (Gen. 10:25) Another reason is the fact that the Bible says that "every mountain and island were moved out of their places." (Rev. 6:14) The other reason is the undeniable fact that the continents as viewed on a world map appear as pieces of a puzzle that would quite well fit together.

At the end of the first day of creation, the world was unformed and void, *i.e.*, it was not perfect. But as God continued His handiwork, at the end of the fifth day He had a perfect world. He had the waters divided from the land area, the sun and moon were giving light, the plants and animals were finished, and He saw that it was all good. Then on the sixth day He created a perfect man—Adam—and him a helpmate, Eve.

When God was preparing to create Adam, He said "let us"—apparently speaking to His only begotten son, Jesus Christ—"make man in our image, after our likeness. . ." (Gen. 1:26). Being created in the image and likeness of God simply means that man would consist of *body, soul,* and *spirit* (I Thess. 5:23). Man would be in a trinity as God is in a trinity. The trinity of God is being the Father, the Son, and the Holy Spirit. Not fewer than three times in the New Testament, the trinity of God is referred to as the "Godhead." (Acts 17:29; Rom. 1:20; and Col. 2:9)

After God had created the animals and gave them life, He created man. There is one major difference between the animal kingdom and man. God gave the man—Adam—the "breath of life and he became a living soul." (Gen. 2:7) This is the creative act that separates mankind from the animal kingdom. No animal was given the breath of life. Therefore, man is an eternal being—never ceasing to exits—whereas animals do not have a soul and are not eternal beings.

III

The Introduction of Sin

Sin is a transgression of God's commandments or laws.

At some time an angel decided that he would do his will rather than God's. The Bible does not tell us exactly when this event occurred; however, it is described to us by Isaiah at 14:12 thus: "How art thou fallen from heaven O Lucifer, son of the morning! How art thou cut down to the ground, which weaken the nations!" Isaiah goes on to relate what led to Satan's (Lucifer's) downfall and reveals when sin began. When Lucifer said "I will" (Isa. 14:13) he rejected God's will and charted his own course. Lucifer said that he would "ascend into heaven, .. .exalt my throne above the stars of God, . . . [and] sit also upon the mount of the congregation,. . . ." (Isa. 14:13-14) I believe that it would actuate to say that this act of Lucifer was the first sin ever committed against the will of God.

Satan is recognized as a liar. (John 8:44) He lied to Eve. God told Adam and Eve that they should not eat of the tree of knowledge or touch it, and if they did they would die. (Gen.

3:1 and 3) But the serpent, *i.e.*, Satan, told them that they could eat of it and not die. (Gen. 3:4)

I have found it very interesting that Satan quoted what God had said to Adam and Eve word for word except for one important fact—he added the word "not." God had said that if they eat, they would die. Satan said that if they eat, they would *not* die. And he has been adding to and subtracting from and misquoting the word of God ever since.

When Adam and Eve ate of the forbidden fruit, they passed a death sentence upon themselves and all future generations of the world. It is therefore no mystery that St. Paul wrote that "the wages of sin is death; . . ." (Rom. 6:23) No truer statement could ever have been written.

The fact that man turned to his own ways and rebelled against God, he could not sliver God love for His creation. After Adam and Eve had eaten the forbidden fruit, "they heard the voice of the Lord God walking in the garden in the cool of the day: . . ." (Gen. 3:8) They tried to hide themselves because they were ashamed of their nakedness. Civilized peoples of the world have been covering themselves with clothes, skins or something every since.

Man having been created as a "living soul," must seek something higher than himself for an anchor in life. And man is in a miserable state of affairs without a god of some sort in his life.

We see a manifestation of man's troubled heart in the sons of Adam and Eve. Cain and Abel. After a period of time, Cain and Abel obviously wanted to find favor with God. Cain brought a fruit "offering unto the Lord." (Gen. 4:3) And Abel brought an offering "of the firstlings of his flock. . . ." (Gen. 4:4)

God was not pleased with Cain offering and rejected it. But God accepted Abel's; apparently Abel brought of the very best that he had to offer to God. Then Satan used a very evil trait—jealousness--to cause Cain to kill his brother Abel. This is the first recorded murder.

The soul within man has a spiritual hungry that he will always seek to fill. The hunger is visible in any people of the world. It is visible in the tribes of darkest Africa where they have their chants and dances. It was present in the Native Americans and their desire of the "Great Spirit." It is this hunger of men's souls that have given rise to all of the false and pagan religions of the world. It is without doubt that it was the hunger of the soul that led Cain and Able to offer up their offerings.

Today there are two false and evil religions sweeping the world. In the Middle East it is Islam, and in America and the West it is Liberalism. And unless they are stopped, they are going to lead to total destruction of the whole world. There is only one thing that will stop these evil and destructive forces—a return to God and his word. America and the West need a revival.

Christianity is a religion of life. The religions of Islam and Liberalism are religions of death. Both have led to the deaths of millions of people. And matters are growing worse and worse because people are looking to world leaders and politicians for answers and solutions to the world's problems. They will find no answers. The answer and the only answer to be found is in the Holy word of God. America and the West must repent of their sins. We do not need more to laws to control people's behavior. We need the spirit of Christ living within the hearts and souls of men and ministers preaching the word of God.

This unique anatomy of man is no doubt what led Christ to say: *"Blessed are they which do hunger and thirst after righteousness: for they shall be filled."* (Matt. 5:6) And to say, *"where your treasure is, there will your heart be also."* (Matt. 6:21) And also to teach that some would be given to: *"the cares of this world, and the deceitfulness of riches, and the lust of other things. . . ."* (Mark 4:19) And to say: *"Lay not up for yourselves treasures upon earth, where moth and rust doth corrupt, and where thieves break through and steal: But lay up for yourselves treasures in heaven, where neither moth nor rust doth corrupt, and where thieves do not break through and steal:* (Matt. 6:19—20).

It is easy to see that in the world today many, many people do not have their minds on righteousness and seeking to deposit their assets in heaven. There is a simply reason for that: they are deceived by Satan.

After God had created Adam and he had fallen from God's good graces by disobeying God and eating of the forbidden fruit, God still loved him.

King David was perplexed by God's love for man: He posed the question: "What is man that thou art mindful of him?" (Ps. 8:4) Then goes to say: "For thou has made him a little lower than the angels, and has crowned him with glory and honor. Thou madest him to have dominion over the works of thy hands; thou hast put all things under his feet." (Ps. 8:5-6) Apparently King David could not understand why God loved man so much after man had sinned and rejected Him. But God did love man. He loved man enough to send His only begotten son, Jesus Christ, to this world as sacrificial lamb to die for the sins of the world.

Man is the most unique creature of God's creation in several ways. Only man has a conscience. Animals do not grieve over deeds they do. There has been no increase of knowledge in the animal kingdom. Animals are no more intelligent today than their like kind were thousands of years ago. But man's knowledge has geometrically increased in all sorts of fields like engineering, medicine, electronics, space, etc. This vast knowledge increase has come from God. God's last days' message to Daniel was that "knowledge shall be increased." (Dan. 12:4).

After the fall of Adam and Cain killed Abel, sin began to spiral out of control and continued for the next ten generations—from Adam to Noah. God was going to wipe mankind off the face of the earth. But Noah found favor in with God. He was directed to build an ark to save him and his family.

However, it was not long until man got into sin again. After the flood, Noah got drunk and was seen by his son Ham, and again the curse of sin was upon mankind. In the ninth generation after Noah, God raised up Abram—who became Abraham. Abraham was a righteous man because he believed God. (Rom. 4:3) He received "an inheritance" because he obeyed God. (Heb. 11:8) "Sara herself received strength to conceive seed, and was delivered of a child when she was past age, because she judged him faithful who had promised." (Heb. 11:11)

"By faith Enoch was translated that he should not see death; . . .[because] he pleased God." (Heb. 11:5) And Moses "refused to be called the son of Pharaoh's daughter; [c]hoosing rather to suffer affliction with the people of God, than to enjoy the pleasures of sin for a season." (Heb. 11:24—25)

All of the above named individuals, and others, received justification because of faith and obedience to the will of God.

The apostle Paul said, "without faith it is impossible to please him [God]:" (Heb. 11:6)

The only way for mankind to have a relationship with God is by faith.

God's people were enslaved in Egypt. Repentance brought them relief. When they cried out to God, he raised up Moses to lead them out. When they reached the land of Canaan, God gave Moses the law for them to obey. But the law in and of itself was a form of bondage (see: Gal. 2:4).

God sent His *only begotten* son to this world to deliver the peoples of the world from the bondage of the law of Moses and from sin.

IV

The Christ

For hundreds of years the prophets had written about a Savior coming into the world. Isaiah wrote that "Behold a virgin shall conceive, and bear a son, and shall call his name Immanuel." (Isa. 7:14) And that He (Christ) would be "despised and rejected of men, a man of sorrows, and acquainted with grief." (Isa. 53:3) He also wrote that "every one that thirsteth, come ye to the waters, and he that hath no money, come ye, buy, and eat, yea, come, buy wine and milk without money and without price." (Isa. 55:1)

Malachi spoke of the coming of Christ by his prophecy of the coming of John the Baptist. He said, "I will send my messenger, and he shall prepare the way before me: and the Lord whom ye seek, shall suddenly come to his temple, even the messenger of the covenant, . . ." (Mal. 3:1)

Malachi's prophecy had been written about four hundred years before John the Baptist arrived. Malachi was the last of the Old Testament prophets and, therefore, God had no direct contact with mankind by a prophet for the four hundred years between Malachi and John the Baptist.

When John the Baptist came preaching repentance, he was "clothed with camel's hair . . ." and he ate "locusts and wild honey; And preached, saying, There cometh one mightier than I after me, the latches of whose shoes I am not worthy to stoop down and unloose. I indeed have baptized you with water: but he shall Baptist you with the Holy Ghost." (Mark 1:6—8).

V

The Life and Ministry of Christ

When Christ was born in the Bethlehem in Judea in 4 B.C., Herod was the King of Judea, and Augustus was the emperor of Rome. All emperors of Rome were known as Caesar until AD 96.

Except for the encounter with the doctors recorded in Luke's gospel (2:46-47) the disciples say nothing of Christ's life until he is baptized by John the Baptist and he begins his ministry. However, other sources of history have much to say and some are annexed in the Appendix.

By the time Christ began his ministry, the whole area of Judea and Jerusalem had fallen to the Romans and had been annexed into the Roman Emperor. Tiberius (AD 14—37) was the emperor of Rome and Pontius Pilate was Rome's provincial governor of the Judea and Samaria providences.

The Jews that hated Jesus and demanded his crucifixion were the Sanhedrin which made up the supreme council and court. They consisted of seventy-one priests, and scribes and elders.

Considering his behavior prior to his conversion to Christianity, the apostle Paul was most likely a Sanhedrin. The apostle Paul was by birth a Jew. He was also a Roman citizen, a very coveted position of the time. Non-citizens were willing to pay great prices for Rome citizenship, including subjecting themselves to slavery for long periods of time.

Jesus began his ministry by commanding the people to "[r]epent for the kingdom of God is at hand." (Matt. 4:17) Then Jesus and his mother were at a marriage in Galilee and his mother told Him that they had no wine. (John 2:1 and 3) His mother told the servants, "Whatsoever he saith unto you, do it." (John 2:5) He told them to *"[f]ill the waterpots with water."* (John 2:7) This was Jesus' first miracle—turning the water into wine.

Nicodemus, a ruler of the Jews came to "Jesus by night and said unto him, Rabbi, we know that thou art a teacher come from God; for no man can do these miracles that thou doest, except God be with him." (John 3:2) Jesus told him, *"Except a man be born again, he cannot see the kingdom of God."* (John 2:3)

Nicodemus had a problem understanding how a man could be born again. Jesus disclosed to Nicodemus—a man well versed in the law that God had given Moses and how God had instructed Moses to put a serpent on a pole for the healing of the people (Num. 21:8–9)—that he, too, would be lifted up, *i.e.*, crucified on a cross. Jesus went on to tell Nicodemus that *"whosoever believeth in him should not perish, but have eternal life."* (John 3:15)

Then Jesus spoke the most famous scripture in the New Testament: *"For God so loved the world, that he gave his only begotten Son, that whosoever believeth in him should not perish, but have everlasting life."* (John 3:16)

Jesus had only approximately three years' time on this earth to accomplish His mission. His purpose was to fulfill the law and to bring forth the grace age—better known as the church age. He came to open the door of salvation to the whole world and to offer himself as a sacrifice for man's sins.

The apostle Paul was a Jewish lawyer that understood the law of Moses well. In his writings, he expanded upon the teachings and purpose of Christ's coming into this world. He wrote: "For if the blood of bulls and of goats, and the ashes of an heifer sprinkle the unclean, sanctifieth to the purifying of the flesh: How much more shall the blood of Christ, who through the eternal Spirit offered himself without spot to God, purge your conscience from dead works to serve the living God?" (Heb. 9:13–14)

The primary purpose of Christ's coming to earth was to offer himself as a lamb "without spot") as a sacrifice for mankind's sins. During the approximately three years of His ministry, He mostly devoted His time to teaching His disciples enabling them to carry His gospel to the world after He returned to heaven. He preached repentance as a condition of salvation. (Mark 1:15)

He also performed many good works. He healed the sick, opened the eyes of the blind, and set an example of righteousness for all peoples of the world to follow.

Christ's public life began when he was baptized by John the Baptist. Then he went into the wilderness and was tempted by the devil for forty days. Then he called Peter and Andrew to be disciples. (Matt. 4:18) When he saw a multitude of people gathering, He went "up into a mountain." (Matt. 5:1) And his disciples "Came unto him." (Matt. 5:2).

In large measure the people rejected him and his teachings; however, multitudes also sought him and recognized him as the promised king. His ministry ended by him being crucified on the cross and shedding his blood for the forgiveness of peoples' sins. They "clothed him with purple, and platted a crown of thorns and put it about his head." (Mark 15:17) They clothed him in purple and put a crown of thorns on his head to humiliate, mock, and shame him by implying that he was claiming to be the emperor of Rome—the King. Christ had identified the rich man whom had lifted his eyes up in hell as being a emperor of Rome. (Luke 16:19) Only the emperor wore purple.

After the crucifixion and resurrection, he remained on earth for forty days after his resurrection teaching his disciples. Then he ascended into heaven. He directed his disciples that they should go to Jerusalem and wait for the promised Holy Ghost to come. Ten days after he ascended into heaven, the Holy Ghost came upon them and the church age began.

The peoples of the world had been separated by various religious and racial barriers for thousands of years, all rooted in sin. Christ broke down all walls of partitions and offered salvation to the whole world. His only requirements for salvation were *repentance* and *belief*. He commanded his disciples to go into all the world and teach (Matt. 28:20) and preach (Mark 16:15) the gospel.

VI

The Church

There will be four definitions of the church as used in this discourse: 1) a church building; 2) the Catholic Church of Rome; 3) a congregation of people involved with a local church building; and 4) the group of believers that will be called out of this world at the return of Christ and also known as his "bride." (Rev. 19:9; 21:9)

The local congregations have a duty to provide a place of worship. Apostle Paul advised the local churches to not forsake "the assembling of ourselves together, . . ." (Heb. 19:25). The local congregations also have a duty to care for the widows (Acts 6:1–7), to preach to the believers, *"Feed my sheep."* (John 21:16–17), and to preach the gospel to unbelievers, *"Go ye into all the world. And preach the gospel to every creature."* (Mark 16:15)

The church age began on the day of Pentecost—fifty days

after Christ's resurrection and ten days after his ascension into heaven.

The disciple had obeyed the instructions of Christ and had gone to Jerusalem to stay until the Holy Ghost came. On the day of Pentecost the eleven remaining disciples—Judas who had deceived Christ and handed him to the Romans, had killed himself—casts lots to determine who would be chosen to replace Judas. The lot fell on Matthias.

The disciples had gone into the upper room alone with approximately one hundred and twenty other persons, including Mary the mother of Jesus, and the Holy Ghost fell upon them and they spoke with other tongues. There were people in Jerusalem from every nation "and they heard the gospel in their own language." (Acts 1:14—26) This is the first recorded history of the descendants of Ishmael having an opportunity to become members of the family of God. Many believed and about three thousand souls were added that day. Others did not believe and not long afterward, they committed the first persecution of the apostles and disciples by stoning Stephen to death. (Acts 6:8—15; 7:54—60)

Following the martyr of Stephen, the apostles and disciples scattered abroad and continued preaching the gospel. (Acts 8:4)

The gospel rapidly advanced throughout the region, and churches soon sprung up in different cities, *e.g.*, Corinth, a sea port in Greece; Galatia, a city in Spain; Colosse, a location in Rome; and Thessaloniki, in central Macedonia. And Christianity had spread as far as Damascus in a relatively short period of time.

One of the persecutors of Stephen was Saul of Tarsus. He had obtained authority from the high priest in Jerusalem to go to Damascus and arrest any disciples—men or women—and bring them to Jerusalem. But on the road to Damascus he was blinded by a bright light and was personally spoken to by Christ and ordained to take the gospel to the Gentiles. (Acts 9:1—15)

After the conversion of Saul of Tarsus, Barnabas was sent by the church at Jerusalem to take the gospel to Antioch. Barnabas went to Tarsus seeking Saul and they went to Antioch and preached the gospel to the Gentiles and those that believed were called Christians. (Acts 11:19–26)

Saul of Tarsus became known as St. Paul (Acts 13:9) and later preached the gospel to the pagans at Rome.

The persecution of the disciples and Christians continued for approximately two hundred and fifty years. The Christians received relief when the Roman Emperor Constantine (AD 280–337) became a Christian in AD 312 and Christianity became the official religion of Rome under emperor Theodosius in AD 380. Emperor Constantine built the Church of the Holy Sepulcher in Jerusalem and it was a Christian city until taken by the Muslims in AD 638. As the Christians Christianized Rome, the Romans Romanized the church. The evidence of which is still visible today by the celebration pagan holidays, etc.

The door of the gospel unto salvation had been opened to the people of Arabia (Acts 2:11) on the day of Pentecost. However, in large measure they continued to worship idols and animistic spirits until AD 610 when Mohammed (AD 570–632) claimed to have received a revelation from the archangel Gabriel that he had been selected to be a prophet. The new prophet attracted a large following and aroused hostilities in Mecca where the inhabitants worshiped a black stone called the Kaaba—allegedly over the burial place of Hagar—Abraham's bond woman—and her son, Ishmael. The hostilities between Mohammed and the people of Mecca led to war in AD 610 and Mecca soon surrendered to him and his followers. Other battles and agreements with other cities and tribes rendered Mohammed supreme in Arabia.

Mohammed advocated a "holy war" against those who refused to agree with his religion. And within one hundred years, the Muslim religion had spread northeast to Syria in West Asia, and westward across Africa to Algeria and Tunisia. Jerusalem fell to the Muslims in AD 638 and remained under their control until taken by the Crusaders in 1099. It was retaken by the Muslins eighty-four years later in 1187 and remained under their control until it was taken by the British in 1917.

In the meantime, the Catholic Church enjoyed great success under King Charlemagne of Frankland. He took Christianity to the area now know as France, Belgium, The Netherlands, Germany, Austria, Switzerland, northern Italy, Poland, Hungary, and Yugoslavia. Pope Leo III proclaimed him head of the Holy Roman Empire in AD 800.

The Muslims engaged in one of the most barbaric persecutions of Christians ever recorded beginning in AD 614. Their barbaric behavior eventually led to the Crusades.

By the time of the crusades, the Roman Emperor had fallen and Rome was under the control of the church. Therefore, the crusades were not wars between the Muslims and Catholics *per se*, but rather between the Muslims and the government of Rome, which was controlled by the Catholics, *i.e.,* the Romanized church.

The first Crusade (1096–09) under Pope Urban II (1088–1099) and preached by Peter the Hermit resulted in thousands of Muslims being killed and reclaimed Jerusalem in 1099.

The second (1147–49) occurred under Pope Eugene III (1145–1153) and preached by St. Bernard on the fall of Edessa to the Turks (1144) and was led by Louis VII of France and Emperor Conrad of Germany.

The third (1189–92) preached by Pope Clement (1187–1191)–after the fall of Jerusalem (1187)–was led by Philippi II of France, Richard I of England and Frederick Barbarossa of Germany.

The fourth (1202-04) was instigated by Pope Innocent III (1198–1216). Constantinople was taken and the Latin Kingdom of Constantinople was established until 1261.

The fifth (1218-21) proclaimed by Pope Innocent III failed.

The sixth (1228–29) was led by Emperor Frederick II secured Jerusalem, Bethlehem and Nazareth by a treaty.

The seventh (1248–54) proclaimed by Pope Innocent IV (1243–54) in 1244 after the fall of Jerusalem (1244) was led by Louis IX of France who was taken prisoner and lost Damietta.

The eighth (1270) was led by Louis IX and he died on an expedition in Tunis.

The Crusades were judged to be failures, but they strengthen the power and prestige of the pope and Rome by increasing trade with the East. They in no wise curbed the abuse of Christians by the Muslims.

The annuals of history are well documented with horror stories of rapes, mutilations and murders of Christians by the bloody hands of Muslims. In 1459, Pope Pius II said that Mohammed was a false prophet.

The Catholic Church was not without its own sin. Several of the church's teachings were contrary to the gospel of Christ. It had drafted far a field from the gospel as preached by St. Paul in Rome in the first century.

In 1483 Martin Luther was born. In 1505 he entered the Augustinian monastery and by 1507 he was a priest. In 1508 he began a theological teaching career at Wittenberg University. He was influenced by a fellow teacher, Johann Staupitz, who died in 1524, and succeeded him as a professor of biblical theology in 1512. Becoming concerned about his own and his parishioners' fate, be began an intense study of the Bible. He was determined to find exactly what God demanded of man for his saving grace. He found the answer to his pressing question in St. Paul's gospel to the Romans: "The just shall live by faith." (Rom. 1:17)

Jesus had told Nicodemus that *"Ye must be born again."* (John 3:7)

After making his new discovery of what God required of sinners to be saved, here is how Luther described his experience: "All at once I began to understand the justice of God as that by which the just live by the gift of God, which is faith: that passive righteousness which the merciful God endures us in the form of faith, thus justifying, rendering us just. . . . At this I experienced such relief and easement, as if I was reborn and had entered through open gates into paradise itself."

Luther was also chagrined because the Dominican friar

Teazel of Germany was selling indulgences on the promises of almost anything to the purchasers—including release of souls from purgatory and forgiveness for transgressions—to raise money to rebuild St. Peter's basilica.

On the 31st day of October 1517, Luther posted his famous Ninety-five Theses on the door of the Castle church in Wittenberg, Germany. All he intended to do was to spark a debate regarding justification by faith. Rather he created a firestorm! He immediately attracted a large group of supporters. An assembly of the church known as the Diet of Worms ordered Luther's seizure and he was excommunicated in 1521. The elector of Saxory of Wittenberg Castle protected him from being seized and while he was in the castle, he began his German translation of the Bible.

Luther further condemned the Catholic Church when on the 6th day of September 1520, he wrote a letter to Pope Leo X, that included the following stinging indictment: ". . .[T]he Church of Rome, formerly the most holy of all Churches, has become the most lawless den of thieves, the most shameless of all brothels, the very kingdom of sin, death, and hell; so that not even the antichrist, if he were to come, could devise and addition to its wickedness."

Luther's reformation movement led to the Protestant churches of the world today. Before his death in 1546, he provided the basic creed for the Lutheran church.

Ulrich Zwingli (1484—1531) established a reform movement in Switzerland agreeing with Luther on many points but disagreeing with him on the retention of a Catholic theology of the real presents of Christ in the Eucharist,--*i.e.*, the sacrament of Communion of breaking of bread and taking of wine—(Cf. 1st Cor. 11:23—25)—viewing it as a symbol or memorial of Christ. After Zwingli's death, the reform movement in Switzerland was led by John Calvin (1509—64). His movement in Switzerland spread to France, Germany and other parts of Europe and on to New England and the colonies, and finally to the establishment of the Presbyterian churches in America.

A third branch of reformers which totally rejected the Catholic doctrine regarding the sacraments was known as the

Anabaptists. The leading theologian of that movement was Menno Simons (1496–1561).

The Mennonite churches of today originated from the Anabaptist movement.

The Methodist Church originated from a movement led by John Wesley (1703–91) in the Church of England—not because of doctrine disagreement but-- because of efforts of King Henry VIII to assert jurisdiction over the church.

Some Baptists trace their roots back to John the Baptist, others to the Anabaptists. The first Baptist Church in America was founded by Roger Williams at Providence, R.I., in 1639.

Many other protestant churches and evangelical organizations and associations have been established in America and other parts of the world since the Reformation events began by Martin Luther. The churches and evangelical organizations of America have taken the gospel of Jesus Christ to all parts of the world.

The Catholic's doctrine remains in conflict with the gospel of Christ on, at least, two major points: 1) Indulgences—the forgiveness of sin. Christ never said or in any wise implied that he was granting authority to his apostles or disciples or the church to forgive sin. The only authority that any man has to forgive sin is against those who trespass against him. And God's forgiveness of our sins is predicated upon our forgiveness of those whom trespass against us. Christ said: *"[F]orgive, if ye have ought against any: that your Father also which is in heaven may forgive you your trespasses. But if ye do not forgive, neither will your father which is in heaven forgive your trespasses."* (Mark 11:25-26); and 2) the Catholics believe that their salvation depends upon their works on this earth. This doctrine is contrary to the gospel of Christ as discovered by Martin Luther.

VII

The Coming End of the Church Age

Christ spoke a lot about the church age coming to an end. He told his disciples that he would go away and prepare a place for them and that he would *"come again, and receive you unto myself; that where* I am *there ye may be also."* (John 14:2—3)

Jesus had come unto his own people, *i.e.*, the Jews, and they had rejected him. He was saddened and disappointed by their behavior. He said: *"O Jerusalem, Jerusalem, thou that killest the prophets, and stonest them which are sent unto thee, how often would I have gathered thy children together, even as a hen gethereth her chickens under her wings, and ye would not. Behold, your house is left unto you desolate."* (Matt. 23:37—38)

Then the disciples wanted to show him the buildings of the temple. He told them there: *"There shall not be left here one stone upon another, that shall not be thrown down."* (Matt: 24:--2)

Soon after he had made these statements, his disciples asked him a three-fold question: 1) "when shall these things be[(?); 2] and what shall be the sign of thy coming [(?); and 3] and of the end of the world." (Matt. 24:3)

Not many days hence, the Jews had the option of asking Pontius Pilate to release Jesus or another prisoner. Pilate asked them, "Whom will ye that I release unto you? Barabbas or Jesus which is called the Christ?" (Matt. 27:17) The Jews demanded the release of Barabbas and the crucifixion of Christ. (Cf. Matt. 27:21—22) "Then answered all the people, and said, His blood be on us, and on our children." (Matt. 27:25)

The Jews demanded a thief and robber be released and Christ to be crucified. And thieves and robbers and murders have been chasing the Jews all over the world ever since.

Jesus answered the disciples' questions: First the temple would be destroyed. This event occurred a little less than forty years later when the Roman Emperor Vespasian had his son Titus destroy Jerusalem in AD 70 and the Jews did not have an inch of land on the face of the earth to call their home until nearly nineteen hundred years later in 1948. And they have been at war ever since trying to hold onto it.

The Jews lost their country to Nebuchadrezzar in 586 B.C. and were carried off to Babylon. Daniel was among the captives. Ezekiel was already in Babylon ministering to he captives of Judah, which had been lost to Nebuchadrezzar in 597 B.C. The Jews were allowed to return to Jerusalem in 538 B.C.

The Babylonians destroyed the temple built by Solomon in 586 B.C. The second temple built under the guidance of Haggai and Zechariah, and others, (Hag. 1:1) was finally complete in 516 B.C. This temple was remodeled by Harold the Great and this work was still in progress at the time of Christ and had been for forty-six years (John 2:2) and was completed in A.D. 64 only to be destroyed by Titus in A.D. 70.

In an over simplified chronicle the other events he spoke about to occur are: 1) warning to not be deceived; 2) false prophets coming in his name; 3) wars and earthquakes; 4) delivering up the disciples to be killed; 5) false prophets; 6) destruction of Jerusalem; 7) saying here or there is Christ; and 8) as the light comes out of the sky, he would return.

Satan wasted no time in trying to deceive the early believers. We see this abundantly clear in St. Paul's letters to the churches. One of the problems was at the churches at Galatia. They were getting entangled with the law. St. Paul made it clear to them the sanctification is through grace and not the law. (Gal. 5:16—24) At the church of Corinth, they were confused about baptism. St. Paul set the record straight: He came "not to baptize, but to preach the gospel." (I Cor. 1:17)

All or nearly all of the apostles were killed and Christians have been killed in many places for their faith.

The forthcoming of false prophets and the destruction of Jerusalem go hand in hand. Christ spoke of the *"abomination of desolation, spoken of by Daniel the prophet, stand in the holy place, (whosoever readeth, let him understand:)"* (Matt. 24:15).

It seems and I believe that Christ's reference to Daniel refers to Daniel chapter 11 verses 21 through 45. It appears that the prophecy of Daniel was foretelling the coming of Mohammed and his rise to great power. Verse 31 mentions the polluting of the sanctuary of strength, taking away the daily sacrifice, and placing the abomination that maketh desolate. The Muslims wrecked Jerusalem in AD 638 and built the Dome of the Rock in AD 691-02 on the site where Solomon's Temple had stood until destroyed by Titus in AD 70, under the Roman Emperor Vespasian who served from AD 69—79.

Verse 36 says: "The king shall do according to his will; and he shall exalt himself, and magnify himself above every god, and shall speak marvelous things against the God of gods, and shall prosper till the indignation be accomplished: for that is determined shall be done."

There are several key phases in this verse: 1) "he shall exalt himself, and magnify himself above every god," this is exactly what Mohammed did. He held himself out to be the last prophet after Jesus and his word to be the final arbitrator on the word of God as revealed to him. Therefore, this phase is consistent with Mohammed's behavior. 2) he "shall speak marvelous things against the God of gods, and shall prosper till the indignation be accomplished:" If Mohammed and his religion is a true representation of God, then God must be determined to be a rapist, murderer, liar, and a God of hate and repression, to name only a few of his evil traits. And it would establish that God had made a complete reinvention of himself, because he had never in all history been as this before. And 3), he "shall prosper." Mohammed and his followers have enjoyed marvelous prosperity; notwithstanding a lot of it have been the fruits of wars, thefts, robbery, etc. And a lot of it is the fruit of God's covenant with Arabham.

God told Abraham that his seed would be as the stars of heaven (Cf. Gen. 15:5). Then after Sara had evicted Hagar out of her and Abraham's home and she was in the wilderness, an angel of the Lord appeared unto her and told her she was with child and to name him Ishmael (Cf. Gen. 16:6--11). The angel told that he would "multiply thy seed exceedingly, that it shall not be numbered for multitude." (Gen. 16:10) Then the angel told Hagar the kind of man Ishmael would become: "And he will be a wild man; his hand will be against every man, and every man's hand against him; and he shall dwell in the presence of all his brethren." (Gen. 16:12)

Daniel's prophecy also says: "And he shall plant the tabernacles of his palace between the seas in the glorious holy mountain; yet he shall come to his end, and none shall help him." (Dan. 11:45)

As recorded by Matthew, Christ explained the forthcoming events to his disciples. First, he foretells them of the *"abomination of desolation, spoken of by Daniel the prophet. . . ."* Then he tells them what to do when the event—the destruction of Jerusalem—occurs, i.e., *"flee into the mountains:"* etc.,(Matt. 24:15–16). This is, I believe, referring to the destruction of Jerusalem which occurred in AD 70.

The Christ mentions *"stand in the holy place, . . ."* (verse 15). This, I believe, is referring to Mohammed's Muslim army overrunning Jerusalem and building the Dome of the Rock temple.

The prophecy of Daniel seems to clearly point to the rise of Mohammed and his Muslim faith. Daniel said, "And arms shall stand on his part, and they shall pollute the sanctuary of strength, and shall take away the sacrifice, and they shall place the abomination that maketh desolate." (Dan. 11:31) The Muslims overrun Jerusalem in AD 614 destroyed the churches built by the Christian Roman emperor Constantine, burned the Church of Calvary and the Sepulchre, stole the relics, and reportedly killed more than thirty-three thousand and eight-hundred Christians and Jews.

Daniel goes on saying: "And the king shall do according to his will; and shall exalt himself, and magnify himself above every god, and shall speak marvelous things against the God of gods, and shall prosper till the indignation be accomplished: for that that is determined shall be done." (Dan. 11:36) Once again, Daniel's prophecy is right on point with the historical behavior of Mohammed. Mohammed did according to his will. He exalted himself as being superior to Christ. And the Muslims have undeniably prospered.

Daniel says: "Neither shall he regard the God of his fathers, nor the desire of women, nor any god, for he shall magnify himself above all." (v. 37) Mohammed clearly had no regard for Abraham—a man of great faith and righteous, etc. (Heb. 11)—nor for women. Mohammed's Koran says: "Your wives are like a field. Plow them as often and anyway you wish." (Koran 2:223) And "that husbands should beat their wives. . . as punishment." (Koran 4:24)

Daniel says that this great false prophet will bring on "a time of trouble, such as never was since there was a nation even to that same time: and at that time thy people shall be delivered, every one that shall be found written in the book." (Dan. 12:1) This prophecy indicates that the Muslims are going to bring a lot of trouble to the world, and at that time, God will deliver his people. This event is referred to by ministers and theologians as the "rapture." The word "rapture" is not in the Bible but means a time when believing Christians expect to be resurrected and caught up to meet Christ in the air and go on into heaven.

The great promise here is that "thy people shall be delivered, every one that shall be found written in the book."

Next Christ taught them the parable of the fig tree. When they saw certain things coming to pass to know that it was near, *"even at the doors."* (Matt. 24:33)

Christ was all knowing. He knew that the Jews were going to lose their country and be scattered all over the world. He also knew that the day would come when he would bring them back home. He knew of the prophecy of Ezekiel wherein it had been said approximately six hundred years earlier: "And I will bring you out from the people, and I will gather you out of the countries wherein ye are scattered, with a mighty hand, and with a stretched out arm, and with fury poured out." (Ez. 20:34) "And ye shall know that I am the Lord, when I shall bring you into the land of Israel, into the country for the which I lifted up mine hand to give it to your fathers." (Ez. 20:42)

Christ was basically telling his disciples that when the

Jews were returned to Israel that they would know that: *"This generation shall not pass, till all these things be fulfilled."* (Matt. 24:34)

Many believe as I do that this scripture means that when Israel recovered its country in 1948 that is the generation that will not pass until all be fulfilled. There are several reasons for this belief:

In the next verse, Daniel tells about the coming of Christ and the resurrection of the saints. (v. 2-3)

Looking back to Matthew and Christ's discourse, he said: *"For then* [after the fulfillment of Daniel's prophecy, including the rapture of the Church] *shall be great tribulation . . ."* (Matt. 24:21)

Christ made it very, very clear that he was coming after his church—*i.e.,* bride *"his wife hath made herself ready"* (Rev. 19:7)—and said: *"In my father's house are many mansions: if it were not so. I would have told you. I go to prepare a place for you. And if I go and prepare a place for you, I will come again and receive you unto myself; that where I am, there you may be also."* (John 14:2–3)

Saint Paul also explained how the event would occur in his letter to the Thessalonians: "For the Lord himself shall descend from heaven with a shout, with the voice of the archangel, and with the trump of God: and the dead in Christ shall rise first: Then we which are alive shall be caught up together with them in the clouds, to meet the Lord in the air: and so shall we ever be with the Lord." (1st Thess. 4:16–17)

Christ further explained to his disciples that his coming would be liken to the days of Noah. He said: *"But as the days of Noe* [Greek for Noah] *were, so shall also the coming of the Son of man be."* Then he explained how that some were taken and some were left when the flood came. He explained his coming *"as the lightening cometh out of the east, and shineth even unto the east; so shall also the coming of the Son of man be.* (Matt. 24:27) And then he tells about the events of the great tribulation; and lastly that after the tribulation, how that the sounding of trumpet will *"gather together his elect from the four winds, from one end of heaven to the other."* (Matt. 24:31) This will be the event when he comes to establish his kingdom and rule with his saints for a thousand years. For we "shall be priests of God and of Christ, and shall reign with him a thousand years." (Rev.20:6)

Nevertheless, the advent of the rapture—or second coming of Christ—will be the end of the church age on earth.

VIII

The Coming End of the World

The end of the world is spoken of in great deal in the Book of Revelation. The first three chapters of the Book are mainly devoted to the churches in Asia, which end with a message to *"the church of the Laodiceans."* (Rev. 3:14) And, Christ saying: *"Behold, I stand at the door and knock: if any man hear my voice, and open the door, I will come in to him, and will sup with him, and he with me."* (Rev. 3:20)

Afterwards, John heard a voice which said, "Come up hither, and I will shew thee things which must be hereafter." (Rev. 4:1)

Some of the highlights of the tribulation period-- the period are generally referred as being the period of time between the calling out of the church, *i.e.,* the "Rapture" and the beginning of reign of Christ on the earth—famine, death, anarchy, and a third part of the of the sea becoming blood (Rev. 8:8), etc. However, the worst part of the tribulation will be the "mark of the beast."

John saw "another beast coming up out of the earth; and he had two horns like a lamb, and spake as a dragon." (Rev. 13:11) "And he causeth all, both small and great, rich and poor, free and bond, to receive a mark in their right hand, or in their foreheads: And that no man might buy or sell, save he that had the mark, or the name of the beast, or the number of his name." (Rev. 13:16—17)

St. Paul wrote regarding the forthcoming times: "Let no man deceive you by any means: for that day shall not come, except there come a falling away first, and that man of sin be revealed, the son of perdition." (2 Thess. 2:3) And St. Paul went on and described the "man of sin," and "the son of perdition" as one: "Who opposeth and exalteth himself above all that is called God, or that is worshiped; so that he as God sitteth in the temple of God, shewing himself that he is God." 2 Thess. 2:4)

"And I saw an angel standing in the sun; and he cried with a loud voice, saying to all the fowls that fly in the midst of heaven, Come and gather yourselves together unto the supper of the great God. That ye may eat the flesh of kings, and the flesh of captains, and the flesh of mighty men, and the flesh of horses, and of them that sit on them, and the flesh of all men, both free and bond, both small and great." (Rev. 19:17–18)

"And the beast was taken, and with him the false prophet that wrought miracles before men, with which he deceived them that had received the mark of the beast, and them that worshiped his image. These both were cast alive into a lake of fire burning with brimstone." (Rev. 19:20)

Many bible scholars and theologians believe that the tribulation period will last seven years. Then Christ will bring his kingdom to the world and rule for a thousand years. (Cf. Rev. 20:6)

This will be a period of time when the born again believers will not be here. There will not be any ministers of the gospel here to counsel the people. Satan and his false prophets will have complete control of the world.

After the thousand year reign of Christ, there will be the "great white throne" judgment and the record books will be opened, and "whosoever was not found written in the book of life was cast into the lake of fire." (Rev. 20:15)

CHAPTER NINE

GOD'S PLAN OF SALVATION

There are five requirements for salvation:

1. A person must realize that he is a sinner;
2. He must realize that he cannot do anything to save himself;
3. He must accept, by faith, that Jesus Christ is the son of God.
4. He must repent of his sins; and
5. He must be born again.

A person must realize that he is a sinner:

Paul wrote to the Romans that "all have sinned and come short of the glory of God." (Rom. 3:23) Jesus said, *"there is none good but one, that is, God:"* (Matt. 19:17) John wrote, "If we say that we have no sin, we deceive ourselves, and the truth is not in us." (1st John 1:8) And "If we say that we have not sinned, we make him a liar, and the word of truth is not in us." (1st John 1:10) James, the brother of Jesus wrote, "Therefore, to him that knoweth to do good, and doeth it not, to him it is sin. (James 4:17)

Paul explained how that sin was brought upon the world by Adam's fall. "Wherefore, as by one man sin entered into the world, and death by sin; and so death passed upon all men, for all have sinned." (Rom. 5:12)

It is firmly established by the word of God that all people are sinners and have committed sin.

He must realize that he cannot do anything to save himself

Jesus made it clear during his ministry that he was the way to salvation and besides him, there was no other way. He said, *"I am the way, the truth, and the life: no man cometh unto the Father, but by me."* (John 14:6) *"And as Moses lifted up the serpent in the wilderness, even so must the Son of man be lifted up. That whosoever believeth in him should not perish, but have eternal life."* (John 3:14–15) Jesus made it clear that the only way to obtain salvation was to believe in him.

He must accept, by faith, that Jesus Christ is the son of God

The coming of Jesus Christ into the world was foretold by Isaiah approximately seven to eight hundred years before his birth that "a virgin shall conceive, and bear a son,..." (Isa. 7:14)

An angel appeared to Mary and told her: "thou shalt conceive in thy womb, and bring forth a son, and shall call his name JESUS." (Luke 1:31) And "The Holy Ghost shall come upon thee, and the power of the Highest shall overshadow thee: therefore also that holy thing which shall be born of thee shall be called the Son of God." (Luke 1:35)

He was found faultless by Pilate (Matt. 27:24). He was resurrected from the dead (Matt. 28:7–10), and was with the apostles for forty days, and "speaking of the things pertaining to the kingdom of God." (Acts 1:3) He was seen by more than five hundred other "brethren." (I Cor. 15:6)

Since his resurrection and ascension, he has been seen

by two individuals: Saul of Tarsus/Paul (Acts 9:4) and John (Rev. 1:3).

And lastly, Paul recapped exactly what the faith is that is required for salvation: "For I delivered unto you first of all that which I also received, how Christ died for our sins according to the scriptures: And that he was buried, and that he rose again the third day according to the scriptures." (I Cor. 15:3—4)

He must repent of his sins

Saint John said, "And the word was made flesh, and dwelt among us, (and we beheld his glory, the glory of the only begotten of the Father) full of grace and glory." (John 1:14) He was acknowledged as being the son of God by "a voice from heaven, saying, This is my beloved Son, in whom I am well pleased." (Matt. 3:17)

After he came from the mountain he *"began to preach, and to say, Repent: for the kingdom of heaven is at hand."* (Matt. 4:17) And he said, *"except ye repent, ye shall all likewise perish."* (Mk. 13:3)

When Apostle Paul went to the idol worshiping city of Athens and stood on Mars' hill he told the inhabitants that there had been times when "God winked at" their ignorance, "but now commandeth all men every where to repent." (Acts 17:30)

"For godly sorrow worketh repentance to salvation:" II Cor. 7:10)

"The Lord is. . .not willing that any should perish, but that all should come to repentance." (2 Peter 3:9)

Repentance is *not* boasting of good works or of keeping the Law of Moses. Jesus used a parable to demonstrate the meaning of repentance. He said *"Two men went up into the temple to pray; the one a Pharisee, and the other a publican. The Pharisee stood and prayed thus with himself, God, I thank thee that I am not as other men are, extortioners, unjust, adulterers, or even as this publican. I fast twice in the week, I give tithes of all that I posses. And the publican, standing afar off, would not lift up as his eyes unto heaven, but smote upon his breast, saying, God be merciful to me a sinner. I tell you, this man went down to his house justified rather than the other. . . ."* (Luke 18:10—14)

Another example of repentance is the repentant thief that was crucified with Christ—according to recorded history, the Romans actually crucified somewhere between one and two thousand Jews within the time frame that Christ was crucified—who said, "Lord, remember me when thou comest into thy kingdom. And Jesus said unto him, *"Verily I say unto thee, To day shalt thou be with me in paradise."* (Luke 23:42—43)

He must be born again

A person has no control over his birth. It is an event of life brought about by others. The new birth or being born again of which Jesus spoke is the result of meeting the prerequisites of repentance and faith in Jesus Christ.

The first experience of mass rebirth occurred on the day of Pentecost. When the people saw the manifestation of the Holy Ghost, they asked Peter, "what shall we do?" (Acts 2: 37) They knew Jesus, they had crucified him fifty days ago, they knew that they had committed an awful wrong; therefore, the only prerequisite left for them to do was to repent and be born again. Peter answered their question: "Repent, and be baptized every one of you in the name of Jesus for the remission of sins and ye shall receive the gift of the Holy Ghost." (Acts 2:38)

Peter was one of the apostles who had received the commission from Christ to: *"Go ye therefore and teach all nations, baptizing them in the name of the Father, and of the Son, and of the Holy Ghost."* (Matt. 28:19)

The baptism that Christ preached for the apostles to perform in his commission was a baptism by water. The baptism that Peter preached to the sinners on the day of Pentecost was spiritual baptism, *i.e.,* immersion in; consumed by; and totally committed to the name of Jesus.

Later there was a division in the church at Corinth and Paul told the church that "Christ sent me not to baptize, but to preach the gospel: . . ." (I Cor. 1:17) Paul made it very clear that water baptism did not result in salvation.

Salvation is not a complicated process. When Isaiah prophesied of the coming of Christ, he said: "the eyes of the blind shall be opened, and the ears of the deaf shall be unstopped. Then shall the lame man leap . . . ." (Isa. 35:5—6) Then more importantly, he said regarding salvation, "an highway shall be there, and a way, and it shall be called The Way of holiness; the unclean shall not pass over it, though fools, shall not error therein." (Isa. 35:8)

CHAPTER TEN

THE BENEFITS OF SALVATION

The most important benefit of salvation is avoiding going to hell, which was *"prepared for the devil and his angels:"* (Matt. 25:41), and the second most important benefit of salvation is to have a home in heaven with Christ, as seen by John, "the building of the wall of it was of jasper: and the city was pure gold, like unto clear glass." (Rev. 21:21) Paul's vision of the third heaven was beyond description. This we do know, Paul said, "I knew a man in Christ above fourteen years ago (whether in the body, I cannot tell; or whether out of the body, I cannot tell: God knoweth;) such an one caught up to the third heaven." (II Cor. 12:2) "How that he was caught up into paradise, and heard unspeakable words, which it is not lawful for a man to utter." (II Cor. 12:4)

Other benefits of salvation include these: 1) Joy: Peter described it as "joy unspeakable and full of glory." (1st Peter 1:8) David prayed for the return of the "joy of thy salvation; . . ." (Ps. 51:12); 2) Peace: Paul said: "being justified by faith, we have peace with God through our Lord Jesus Christ:" (Rom. 5:1); 3) Hope: Paul said: "By whom also we have access by faith into this grace wherein we stand, and rejoice in hope of the glory of God." (Rom. 5:2); Patience: Paul said that "tribulation worketh patience and patience, experience, and experience hope." (Rom. 5:3−4); 5) "we shall be saved from wrath through him." (Rom.

5:9); 6) Happiness: David said, "happy is that people, whose God is the Lord." (Ps. 144:5); 7) Liberty: Paul said, "where the Spirit of the Lord is, there is liberty." (II Cor. 3:17); and 8) Love: Love is the true characteristic of Christianity. John said, "We know that we have passed from death until life, because we love the brethren." (1st John 3:14) Paul said that if he did not have love, he was "nothing." (Cf. I Cor. 13:1–13)

Another benefit of salvation is that there will be a family reunion in heaven. When David realized that his son was going to die, he "fasted and wept." (2 Sam. 12:16 and 22) After the child died, David got up "and washed himself, and anointed himself, and changed his apparel, . . . and eat." (v. 20) His servants asked him why his behavior had changed. David said unto them: "But now he is dead, wherefore should I fast? can I bring him back again? I shall go to him, but he shall not return to me." (2 Sam. 12:23)

The pages of history are well stained with the blood of believers and saints that was shed at the hands of evil men. But we also know that when God has poured out his wrath upon the world, as he did with the flood, he saved and protected his people. And when he destroyed the cities of Sodom and Gomorrah, he got his servant Lot and his wife out before the fire and brimstone came down from heaven, but Lot's wife looked back and became a pillar of salt. (Cf. Gen. 19:1–27)

Jesus said: *"But as the days of Noe* [Greek for Noah] *were, so shall also the coming of the Son of* man *be."* (Matt. 24:37) When God sent the flood to destroy the people because of their sins and wickedness, his people was saved from his wrath. His people will be saved during the tribulation period.

His people are to have no fear. He said: *"And there shall be signs in the moon, and in the stars, and upon the earth distress of nations with perplexity, the sea and the waves roaring. Men's hearts failing them for fear, and for looking after those things which are coming on the earth: for the powers of heaven shall be shaken."*

"And when these things begin to come to pass, then look up, and

lift up your heads, for your redemption draweth nigh." (Luke 21:25, 26 and 28)

Christ's last warning to his disciples before his betrayal and crucifixion was: *"And take heed to yourselves, lest at any time your hearts be overcharged with surfeiting, and drunkenness, and cares of this life, and so that day come upon you unawares. For as a snare shall it come on all them that dwell on the face of the whole earth. Watch ye therefore, and pray always, that ye may be accounted worthy to escape all these things that shall come to pass, and to stand before the Son of man."* (Luke 21:34−36)

We can know that when these awful days come that the people−*i.e.*−"kings of the earth, and the great men, and the rich men, and the chief captains, and the mighty men, and every bondman, and every free man, hid themselves in the dens and in the rocks of the mountains; And said to the mountains and the rocks, Fall on us, and hide us from the face of him that sitteth on the throne, and from the wrath of the Lamb: For the great day of his wrath is come, and who shall be able to stand?" (Rev. 6:15−17)

Saint Paul counseled the people as to how to avoid being in this awful situation. He said: "That at the name of Jesus every knee should bow, of things in heaven, and things on earth, and things under the earth; And that every tongue should confess that Jesus Christ is Lord, to the glory of God the Father." (Phil. 2:10−11)

We know that according to the Book of Revelation that within a span of a few years, many ministers of the gospel and theologians believe seven and so do I, that two-thirds' of the world's population will die and the conditions of life will be beyond anything any people has ever seen since the beginning of time, but the children of God have nothing to fear.

The born again believers will only stand before the judgment seat of Christ (Rom.14:10) and only for the purpose of receiving their rewards for the works that they have done for the glory of God. (I Cor. 1:8) However, the ungodly, sinners and unbelievers shall stand in judgment before Almighty God at the "great white throne" judgment and be rewarded with damnation according to their evil deeds. (Rev. 20:11)

The advent of Christ's return and the beginning of the great tribulation period could occur at any time. The signs of the times are evident around the world.

CHAPTER ELEVEN

COMMANDS FOR MANKIND

God has commanding what man is to do and to not do since the beginning of time. And God's blessings for obedience is beyond measure as are the awful consequences for disobedience.

The wise man Solomon said, "Remember now thy Creator in the days of thy youth." (Eccl. 12:1) He went on to comment on how time changes life's events. Time makes life's choices more difficult.

There are two verses of scripture that dictate the current status of each one on earth. The first says: "My spirit shall not always strive with man, . . ." (Gen 6:3), clearly declaring that time is of the essence for doing the will of God; and the second one says: *"In my Father's house are many mansions:"* (John 14:2) and that he has gone to *"prepare a place. . . ."* (John 14:3)

The circumstances of the unrighteous is that God's patience and mercy have not expired, and the circumstances of the righteous is that he has not gotten their mansions finished.

History well documents the wisdom of obedience and faith in God beginning with Abel who offered a more acceptable sacrifice than Cain; because of his faith, Enoch was translated and taken to heaven without dying; Noah avoided death in the flood because of his faith and obedience to God; Abraham and Sara were given a son in their old age because of their faith and obedience; Moses refused to be called the son of Pharaoh's daughter and chose to suffer rather than enjoy the pleasures of sin for a period of time; and the life of the harlot Rahab was spared because of her faith.

Salvation brings peace at the time of death. When Paul knew that he was going to be soon killed, he said: "I have fought a good fight, I have finished my course, I have kept the faith." (2 Tim. 4:7) Paul had been fighting against sin and evil unbelievers since the time of his conversion to faith in Christ. I Ie said, "For we wrestle not against flesh and blood, but against principalities, against powers, against the rulers of the darkness of this world, against spiritual wickedness in high places." (Eph. 6:11) He had fought a good fight because he had never failed to stand for his convictions of what was right and right in the sight of God.

CHAPTER TWELVE

A VISION OF DEATH

The Bible says that: "And it is appointed unto men once to die, but after this the judgment." (Heb. 9:27) The wise man Solomon said: "in the place where the tree falleth, there it shall be." (Eccl. 11:3) It is, therefore, perfectly clear that the next event after death is judgment—before the judgment seat of Christ for the saved, and before the great white throne judgment for the unsaved.

The background material for this chapter is based upon the scriptures and others' accounts that have had what is commonly referred to as "near death experiences," and testimonies of individuals near death.

First, Stephen saw Christ in heaven "standing on the right hand of God" as he was dying (Acts 7:55).

Secondly, Christ told of the death of the beggar. He said: *"There was a certain rich man, which was clothed in purple and fine linen, and fared sumptuously every day: And there was a certain beggar named Lazarus, which was laid at his gate, full of sores. And desiring to be fed with the crumbs which fell from the rich man's table: moreover the dogs came and licked his sores. And it came to pass, that the beggar died, and was carried by the angels into Abraham's bosom: the rich man also died, and was buried; And in hell he lifted his eyes, being in torments, and seeth Abraham afar off, and Lazarus in his bosom. And he cried and said, Father Abraham, have mercy on me, and send Lazarus that he may dip the tip of his finger in water, and cool my tongue, for I am tormented in this flame."* (Luke 16:19—24) Jesus had told his disciples a parable of another rich man, *"saying, The ground of a certain rich man brought forth plentifully: And he thought within himself, saying, What shall I do, because I have no room where to bestow my fruits? And he said, This will I do: I will pull down my barns, and build greater; and there will I bestow all my fruits and my goods. And I will say to my soul, Soul, thou hast much goods laid up for many years; take thine ease, eat, drink, and be merry. But God said unto him, thou fool, this night thy soul shall be required of thee: then whose shall these things be, which thou hast provided?* (Luke 12:16—20)

Death is not an inspiring subject for discussion. People do not like to think about it and other than ministers of the gospel, many do not discuss it in detail. Nevertheless it is inevitable. Therefore, it is important to know something of what happens when it occurs. The Bible makes it very clear that the departed go to either heaven or hell. The word "hell" has four different meanings according to its use in the Hebrew and Greek languages: 1) *hades*: world of the dead; 2) bow of the knee; 3) place of everlasting punishment; and 4) to incarcerate in eternal torment. It is also often referred to as a "pit." For example, an angel opened the "bottomless pit" and demonic locusts came out of the smoke of the pit. (Rev. 9:1—2) And an angel shall bind the Devil and cast him into the "bottomless pit." (Rev. 20:1—3)

We also know that heaven is a place of joy. Paul wrote to the Corinthians, "Eye hath not seen, nor ear heard, neither have entered into the heart of man, the things God hath prepared for them that love him." (I Cor. 2:9)

We know from the scriptures that heaven is a place to be desired and hell is a place to be avoided. Several individuals have had "near death experiences" and a number of books have been written and public discussions via the media regarding them. Some have described their decent toward hell as being a tunnel with demonic creatures reaching for them with long claws, monstrous beasts, etc. Others have described their view of heaven as beautiful scenes and lights, etc.

Others have offered their testimonies of visions. My grandmother related to her family just hours before dying that one of her departed sons had visited her. A six-year-old child announced seeing Jesus within seconds of death.

Testimonies of caretakers of the terminal ill have related the pure horror on the faces of some of the dying, *i.e.*, death masks, and smiles of joy on the faces of the saved.

The Bible as well as other evidence makes it abundantly clear that it is the most important thing in life is to prepare for death. Preparing for death is far more important than preparing for living. The teachings of Christ regarding the two rich men quoted above makes that very clear.

Christ asked: *"For what shall it profit a man, if he shall gain the whole world, and lose his own soul?"* (Mark 8:36) The answer is: Nothing! On the contrary, it is the worst loss that any person could ever suffer.

CHAPTER THIRTEEN

THE STATE OF THE WEST

The West[1] is in trouble for three reasons: 1) the world stands on the threshold of the end of the church age; 2) sin is raging out of control; and 3) churches are failing to preach the gospel. Much of what is occurring in the world is simply the time has come for these things to come to pass.

The Bible says that "Righteousness exalteth a nation: but sin is a reproach to any people." (Prov. 14:34) And "The wicked shall be turned into hell, and all nations that forget God." (Ps. 9:17)

Today sin is on the march across the world at an unprecedented pace. And if history teaches anything it is that those who do not learn from history make the same mistakes as past generations. It is obvious in every area of the world that the players on the world stage have failed to learn from the mistakes of past generations.

Christ referred to his return for the church as being in times not unlike the days of Noah. In the days of Noah before the flood, "wickedness of man was great in the earth, . . . " (Gen. 6:5) And "[T]he earth also was corrupt before God, and the earth was filled with violence." (Gen. 6:11)

Paul said, "This know also that in the last days perilous

times shall come. For men shall be lovers of their own selves, covetous, boasters, proud, blasphemers, disobedient to parents, unthankful, unholy, Without natural affection, trucebreakers, false accusers, incontinent, fierce, despisers of those that are good, Traitors, heady, highminded, lovers of pleasures, more than lovers of God; Having a form of godliness, but denying the power thereof: from such turn away." (2 Tim. 3:1—5)

The West is in trouble because evil is present on every corner The West has forgotten God. A large segment of society is more in love with the creation than the creator. They have invented unto themselves religions—evil religions—that fails to recognize the God of Abraham, Isaac and Jacob.

A few of the more noteworthy sins prevailing in the West include, but are not limited to, the following:

Abortion: Abortion is causing the death of an unborn child. It is, of course, performed for different reasons. Some simply do not want the child. Some do not want to interrupt their lives to care for the child, etc. Abortion is not new.

Abortion was addressed in the Law of Moses in the following manner: "If men strive, and hurt a woman with child, so that her fruit depart from her, and yet no mischief follow: he shall be surely punished, according as the woman's husband will lay upon him; . . . . And if any mischief follow, then thou shall give life for life." (Ex. 21: 22—23) It seems clear enough that if the child was okay, the punishment was rather light. But if the child was lost because of the act of harm, then the punishment was death to the offender.

Granted, we are not under the Law of Moses; however, God has not changed. What was sin under the Law of Moses is still sin today. The ceremonial aspects of the Law of Moses were considered "bondage" and were relieved by Christ's grace.

Abortion or the killing of children in any other manner is murder and prohibited by the Ten Commandments. "Thou shalt not kill." (Ex. 20:13)   However, abortion goes beyond murder. Abortion is in reality a form of sacrifice to whatever the reason for not wanting the child. It is equal to sacrificing a child to an idol. Such behavior was engaged in by Israel and was addressed by David: "yea, they sacrificed their sons and their daughters unto devils, And shed innocent blood, even the blood of their sons and their daughters, whom they sacrificed unto the idols of Canaan: and the land was polluted with blood." (Ps. 106:37–38) And David goes on to say that God "gave them into the hand of the heathen; and they that hated them ruled over them." (Ps. 106:41)

Abortion has become a sacred tenet of liberal politicians. They view it as a sacred right. But in truth it is bringing destruction upon the nations that allow and practice it. Destruction of the nations is a promise from God.

As the Christians stand against the evil of abortion and other national sins, former Vice-President and presidential candidate Al Gore remarked that the Christians were people with an extra chromosome, implying that we Christians were affected with a serious mental disorder known as Down syndrome, which is caused by three copies of the twenty-first chromosome. His remark caused an outrage by parents of Down syndrome children but he still almost won the presidency of the United States.

`Homosexuality: Homosexuality is a very hot topic in our society today. Not only is it wide spread in society, but it is a touchy subject for discussion. Notwithstanding all of the hype, it is an abominable sin.

Some time ago I heard a lady defending homosexuality on a radio program and her argument was to the effect that it was not mentioned in the Bible. As homosexuality, she is correct, it is not. However, in other terminology it is profoundly mentioned. Its practitioners are said to be "without nature affection" (2 Tim. 3:3) and as "men knowing men" (Gen. 19:5) and defined as "wickedness" (v. 7) and it was the cause of fire and brimstone raining down from heaven destroying Sodom and Gomorrah. (Gen. 19:23–24)

I have been blessed with the opportunities of having known some homosexuals and became very friendly with a few. I knew that they were and they knew that I was not. However, getting to know them very well and being able to freely discuss subjects and issues with them without offence, I sought the root of their sexual orientation. I am of the persuasion that it is the result of child abuse of one form or another. For males, it is abuse by the mother, and for females, abuse by the father or another male figure in their young lives. The end result is that the child hates people of his/her opposite gender.

Homosexuality is not a simply problem to deal with or to overcome. God does not wink at homosexuality or any other sin. But he loves homosexuals as he does all sinners and his grace is sufficient for forgiveness.

<u>Idolatry</u>: Idolatry is the worship of any other god except the God of Abraham, Isaac, and Jacob. The first of the Ten Commandments was: "Thou shalt have no other gods before me." (Ex. 20:3)

Idolatry is alive and well in America. One of the principle gods in America is the government. The citizens are given to looking to the government for their needs and wants. And if the government fails to deliver, they are angry and the public officials in Washington and the State Houses hear from them loud and clear.

Another god of idolatry in America is money. The people act as if enough money can solve all problems. The people's dependency on money as their security is a misguided conception. Money cannot buy health or happiness. Many rich people are very unhappy and seek help from psychiatrists and other health care professionals. Money is a false god.

Another form of idolatry is the seeking of peace and happiness. This takes to form of hang-ups without commitments. For example, sports fans. They can talk about the achievements of the players on their team and look forward to the next game and be totally devoted to the games. It also takes the form of sporting events themselves, *e.g.* golf, boating, fishing, etc. These people's lives revolve around the activity.

Another form is political power and authority and other professions. Their lives revolve around gaining more and more power, influence and prestige. These types of people eventually become to believe that the good—as they define good—is pleasing to God and will get them into heaven.

We see this sort of idolatry in such organizations as the National Organization for Women. They are dedicated to keeping abortion legal that it has become like a religion to them. We see the same sort of behavior in organizations such as the Sierra Club, Greenpeace, and the more radical Earth First group. Their philosophies and their dedication to them are clearly their religions.

Idolatry is certainly not new. After God had delivered the children of Israel out of Egypt they could not wait for Moses to come down from the mountain until they demanded Aaron make them a golden calf to worship. (Ex. 32:1—6) And the Israelites continued to get involved with it, including the wise man Solomon. (1 Kings 11:15) Nevertheless, God is never pleased with it. And sin does not go unpunished.

Adultery: Adultery is another sinful practice that is alive and well in America. Adultery is generally defined as being unfaithful to a person to whom a commitment has been made. However, in this discourse, I will address adultery in its spiritual sense rather than in it natural.

Adultery is closely related to idolatry. The difference is idolatry is the worship of a natural thing or image of an object. Spiritual adultery is the forsaking of a commitment to God. The Israelites had a real problem with both adultery and idolatry. God condemned both behaviors in the strongest possible terms.

There is nothing dealing with religion that I find as distasteful as I do attacking churches and criticizing ministers of the gospel. However, my higher calling is to righteousness and truth. And the truth is both churches and ministers are woefully failing to promulgate the truth of the gospel of Jesus Christ. They clearly seem to be more interested in enriching themselves that they are in proclaiming the gospel to the lost and denouncing sin—sins such as I have written about herein.

It is certainly true that believers in Christ have a duty to build churches and support ministers of the gospel. They also have a duty to teach and preach the truth—that Jesus Christ is the way, and the only way, to salvation. Good works will not suffice, giving money to churches and preachers will not suffice. Jesus Christ came into this world to seek and save the lost. There is a heaven to gain and a hell to avoid. He did not come to condemn the world but to save the souls of sinners.

The churches and ministers have to accept the blame for the wide spread belief in our society that people can live their lives without any regard for God or his righteousness and believe that when they die that they will go to heaven. That is a false doctrine. There is not an iota of scripture to support such a doctrine in the Bible.

Another false doctrine being promulgated by churches and ministers is that to receive God's blessings something (money) must first be given, *e.g.*, "seed faith." There is not a single incident recorded in the Bible where this was practiced by the disciples. The only thing required of people to receive God's blessings is *faith*. The gifts and blessings of God are not for sale.

I in no wise suggest that people should not support churches and ministers. They clearly should and will definitely be rewarded for doing so. The Bible says: "He which soweth sparingly shall reap also sparingly; and he which soweth bountifully shall reap also bountifully. Every man according as he purposeth in his heart, so let him give, not grudgingly, or of necessity: for God loveth a cheerful giver." (II Cor. 9:6—7) And "Behold, to obey is better than sacrifice, and to hearken than the fat of rams." (2 Sam. 15:22)

Christ said: *"For where your treasure is, there will your heart be also."* (Luke 12:34) The treasures of this world shall fade away, but what we do for the glory of God will never fade away. Everything that we do for the glory of God here on earth adds to our heavenly treasure. Even as little as a drink of cold water will not go unrewarded (Mark 9:41)

America has become a very greedy nation. Americans in

large measure have put their trust in the silver and gold of this world. A drop of a few points in the stock market creates panic. Every natural disaster is met with additional demands that the government "do something" about it. The nation's motto is "In God We Trust," but in reality the nation really has its trust in money and the government. Words mean nearly nothing. Talk is cheap, anyone can say anything. It is deeds that count.

James said: "shew me thy faith without works, and I will shew thee my faith by my works." (James 2:18) Faith will lead to good works, and if there is no work for God, there is no faith.

America has not learned well from history. When the Europeans settled here they had to know something of history. They had to know about the crusades, the ungodly authority of the pope over the church, and the oppressiveness of the King against the church. Notwithstanding this knowledge, just like the Israelites in the days of Jeremiah, they followed Judah's errors. God had delivered Israelites out of the land of bondage and brought them into a new land. Jeremiah said: "And I brought you into a plentiful country, to eat the fruit thereof and the goodness thereof; but when ye enter, ye defiled my land, and made my heritage an abomination." (Jer. 2:7)

The first major mistake the new settlers made in America was bringing slaves in from Africa. The slaves brought what was then called "Mahometan" religion with them. Some have estimated that ten to twenty percent of the slaves were Muslims.[3] The "new" religion was also called "Mohammedanism."[4]

According to reliable sources of information, Muslims began to migrate to the United States in 1875. Then three major waves of immigrations followed: 1) 1930's; 2) 1947; and 3) 1967.

Islam is reportedly the fastest growing religion in America. Its growth is not limited to African-American heritage. In 1975 there was an estimated 40,000 to 75,000 white Muslims in America.

Islam is an evil and ungodly religion. It was founded by an evil and ungodly man. The prophets of the Old Testament and the apostles and disciples of the New Testament proclaimed that their inspirations came from God. Mohammed, on the other hand, admitted that "Satan spoke satanic verses through his mouth." (Koran 22:52; 53:19—20) Mohammed admitted to being demon possessed. Mohammed was a pedophile and married a nine year old girl when he was fifty-three years old. Islam claims that Allah is God. In reality, Allah is the moon god of Arabs. Islam teaches paganism. Is portrays Allah as a racist, sexist and violent god; and treats women as sexual objects, and allows men to have four or more wives and as many concubines as they wish.

Islam is advancing across the West at an unprecedented pace and causing noticeable problems for the local and national governments. The Muslims want to establish Islamic Shariah law in the United Kingdom. The Chairman of the Commission for Racial Equality (CRE) told BBC News on February 26, 2006, that the UK should "allow people to offend each other," and that the Muslims "who wanted a system of Islamic Shariah law should leave the UK."

Tom Blankley of *The Washington Times* reported on September 12, 2005, that "The threat of radical Islamists taking over Europe is every bit as great to the United States as was the threat of the Nazis taking over Europe in the 1940s."

When God gives a people possession or a blessing and they abuse it or him, he allows the enemy to take it away and imprison those to whom it was given. This is a fact well documented in the Old Testament and the Israelites. Time after time the Israelites were carried off into slavery for disobedience.

Paul addressed this sort of behavior to the Romans and later to Timothy. He said: "Who changed the truth of God into a lie, and worshipped and served the creature more than the Creator, who is blessed forever. Amen. For this cause, God gave them up unto vile affections: for even their women did change the natural use into that which is against nature: And likewise also the men, leaving the natural use of the women, burned in their lust one toward another; men with men working that which is unseemly, and receiving in themselves that recompence of their error which was meet. And even as they did not like to retain God in their knowledge, God gave them over to a reprobate mind, to do those things which are not convenient." (Rom. 1:25–28)

There are at least four definitions of reprobate. It can mean castaway, rejected, a person who pursues evil rather than good, and condemned by God to eternal damnation. They could also be identified as psychopaths, *i.e.*, devoid of conscience.

It is easy to correlate Paul's writings of nearly two thousand years ago with what is occurring before our eyes in America and the West today. Homosexuality is becoming commonplace and HIV is an epidemic in the land. The "wages of sin" is still death.

For lack of condemnation, activities which are clearly sinful are being accepted under the misguided notion of "political correctness" as acceptable in our society. The country is paying the price as well as the perpetrators of the sinful deeds.

Anyone who has the backbone to take a stand and condemn their evil deeds is called derogatory and insulting names, accused of being "politically incorrect," and faulted for not being open minded. They do exactly what Paul said that they would do: "[despise] . . . those that are good." (2 Tim. 3:3)

The sins of the nations are at the root of the United States' and the world's problems. God spoke through his prophet of old and said: "If my people, which are called by my name, shall humble themselves, and pray, and seek my face, and turn from their wicked ways; then will I hear from heaven, and will forgive their sin, and will heal their land." (2 Chr. 7:14) The sin of God's people is not the problem of the world today. God's people are doing a remarkable job of standing against sin. A few of those that are taking a strong stand for righteousness are Dr. James Dobson and his *Focus on the Family* organization, Liberty Counsel, Dr. Jerry Farwell and Liberty University, Trinity Broadcasting Network (TBN) is taking the gospel around the world. The problem lies with liberal politicians and liberal lawyers and liberal judges.

Satan was a snake when he deceived Eve in the garden. He was a snake when he tempted Christ after his forty-day mountain fast (Cf. Matt. 4:2–7), and he is still a snake today. He offered Christ the kingdoms of this world and Christ rejected his offer out-of-hand. However, today Satan's kingdoms are being accepted with open arms by the false prophets and liberal lawyers and others.

Christ said: *"Woe unto you, lawyers! For ye have taken away the key of knowledge: ye entered not in yourselves, and them that were entering in ye hindered."* (Luke 11:52)

No Congress of the United States or any President thereof has ever signed a law banning the Bible or prayer from a public school or the display of the Ten Commandments in public building. Yet it is the law of the law. So how can this be? It is the way it is because liberal judges have determined the right to freedom of religion is freedom from religion. That was not the intent of the Founding Fathers of our country. In fact, the Constitution of the United States specifically denies Congress authority to enact any law regarding religion. The liberal judges have usurped authority which the Constitution does not grant them. The legislative powers is vested in Congress—not the judicatory. This was a recognized fact before the liberals high-jacked our courts and government. Back in 1821 the United States Supreme Court held: "We have no more right to decline the exercise of jurisdiction which is given, than to usurp that which is not given. The one or the other would be treason to the constitution.[5] Treason is an impeachable offense.[6]

The illegal acts go unchallenged because the Congress lacks the wherewithal to confront the judges and impeach them or they support their illegal acts because they agree with their illegal philosophy. The righteous people of the country—commonly referred to as the "Christian Right"—do not like or approve of congress' lack of action. They try to influence who is elected and succeed at times of getting some of the bad actors out. However, more common than not, the newly elected are as bad as those voted out of office. Therefore, little progress is made, and a woefully lack of progress is achieved.

CORPORATIONS AND LABOR UNIONS: These entities are motivated by money. They both imbibe for every penny they can get. The corporations know that they have to sell for the lowest price possible and the less cost of making a widget the lower the price they can sell it. The lower it sells, the more items will be purchased.

The employees know the lower wages the corporations pay the more profit the corporations will realize.

Corporations have in many regards enslaved the labor force of the free world. The labor unions have been formed to resist the corporations' power and influence, and the abuse of laborers.

The labor unions have supported liberal politicians who are friendly to their causes by enacting labor laws that addresses the treatment of laborers by the corporations. The interests of both the corporations and the labor unions are motivated by greed.

One of the most harmful things that labor unions have been able to accomplish is the unionization of school teachers. This opened the door for liberal propaganda to be disseminated to the most vulnerable of the country's future citizens.

The propaganda of liberals and their agenda have not promoted the attributes of God and his directions for the good of mankind. They have taught the theory of evolution as fact. They have promoted their godless religious doctrine of environmentalism. Clearly they are more concerned for the creation than the Creator.

Another one of their pet liberal agendas is the promotion of sex and particularly homosexuality. It is quite evident that their agenda is working very well for them. According to data released by the National Education Association (NEA) a survey taken by the Gay, Lesbian and Straight Education Network (GLSEN) in 2005, thirty-seven point eight percent of students reported physical harassment at school because their sexual orientation—that is more than one-third of the students; and more than twenty-five percent of the students reported physical harassment because of their sexual expression. Another pet agenda of the liberal school authorities is to get "student diversity training" in the schools. In a case in Kentucky the local federal district court ruled that parents *do not* have a right to have their children opt out of the training.[7] It did not matter that the parents objected on religious grounds. Therefore, it is a given of the liberals and teachers' union to openly support homosexuality in the public schools while disregarding the parents' concerns.

The liberals and their supporters do not believe in nor support the constitutional guarantee of "equal protection." They believe in and support "extra" protection for minorities. In their view discrimination on the bases of race, color, sex, and religion is acceptable if the discrimination benefits a minority such as African-Americans, homosexuals, or Muslims.

Righteous people believe in respecting those with whom they disagree. No better example is to be found than the encounter that Christ had with the woman caught in an act of adultery. (John 8:5–11) Jesus did not condone her behavior and neither did he condemn her. He simply told her to *"go, and sin no more"* (v.11). Righteous people do not believe in imposing their beliefs upon others against their will or by force. That is not to say that they do not support enactment of laws regulating morality and vices.

If gambling is legal, they tolerate it; if alcohol is legal, they tolerate it, too. They do not engage in violence and murder in support of their clauses.

Righteous people believe in doing what is right. They believe that a person who does a day's work is entitled to a day's pay, and one who receives a day's pay is obligated to perform a day's work. This is the righteous and godly way of conducting business.

Corporations are a necessary evil. Without them we would have no industrial or manufacturing base. The cost of engineers, designing and manufacturing goods is far too great to be possible for one or a few individuals. Therefore, the funding for industrial development has to be raised by selling stock in corporate entities. And, of course, investors invest money in corporate stock because they expect to earn a profit from their investments.

Juvenile Delinquency: Juvenile delinquency has become a very serious problem in our society. According to the United States Department of Justice, in 2000 there were more one hundred thousand minors arrested for serious violent crimes. That is an outrageous number of children to be involved in such crimes as murder, rape, and serious assault.

There are three main reasons for the children's behavior: 1) the violent shows on television; 2) the availability of illegal drugs and their use and the temptation of money to be earned by dealing in them by children especially in the public schools; and 3) the woefully lack of religious training at home and in the public schools.

Before the modern communications age that the country is in today, children respected each other far more than they do today and they respected older people. Now they have no respect for each other or older people. Television has proven to be a bad teacher of the youth.

Illegal drugs are unrestricted to children because children have money. The illegal drug dealers are in business for the money and it is their only motivation. They have no concern regarding the damage their wares do to the youth.

And lastly, the problem lies with the parents and the lack of proper religious training. For those who are not accustom to attending church, a small percentage of the community's children are taken to church and that small number are not into violence or drugs. They are dedicated students in school. Some are into music and already recording records. Their parents are dedicated to guiding them onto the paths of righteous.

The Bible says: "Remove not the ancient landmark, which thy fathers have set." (Prov. 22:28) Parents who want—truly want—their children to succeed in life take them to church and teach them the ways of righteousness. Parents have an obligation to teach their children right from wrong. This type of training by parents is viewed as bad by the liberals who want to teach other people's children to be acceptable to all sorts of immoral behavior. God did not dictate to the state, the schools, the community or village the responsibility of rearing the community's children. That responsibility rests solely on the shoulders of the parents and the pastors and Sunday school teachers of the local churches.

The ancient landmark of parents devoting time to their children have been cast aside and replaced by the actors of Hollywood serving as the baby-sitters and opinion molders of America's youth. America has lost a generation—or more--of its youth. The youth in America are sometimes referred to as "the throw away generation." This is a rude but true observation of parents' failure to be parents to their children.

Child Abuse: Child abuse is closely related to juvenile delinquency. Child abuse is executed in many different forms. One is neglect of spending time with a child. There is nothing that a child desires more than attention and involvement in whatever interest them. The first thing a child wants to do when it learns a new thing is to show mommy. Every achievement is a big event to a child. To deny a child that sort of attention, is a form of abuse. The attention that a child receives is a demonstration of love. When a child is denied attention it believes that it is not loved. This leads to an introverted personality, inferiority complex, and may later in life lead to a "bullying" personality.

Two working parent homes have deprived children a lot of valuable time with at least one parent, generally the mother. The consequences are well documented and severe. According to the Public Policy Office of the American Psychological Association, ten percent of children and adolescents have serious mental health problems and another ten percent have minor mental health problems. These health problems lead to suicide, substance abuse, and other problems. With one in five or twenty percent of the youth of the nation suffering from mental illnesses, we are dealing with an epidemic.

Another form of child abuse is the notion that children can be expected to act like little adults. The news organizations have well documented incidents of children as young as five years old being arrested for "crimes." Children should be allowed to be children.

The "ancient landmark" of child rearing has been removed from society. This is not a good or wise decision. The Bible has a great deal of instructions for child rearing. The Bible says:

"Train up a child in the way he should go: and when he is old, he will not depart from it." (Prov. 22:6) And, "He that spareth his rod hateth his son: but he that loveth him chasteneth him betimes." (Prov. 13:24)

It is a fact that these scriptures have been misused to justify abuse of children by parents. And this fact was addressed by the Apostle Paul in two of his letters to two different churches. To one he wrote: "And, ye fathers, provoke not your children to wrath: but bring them up in the nurture and admonition of the Lord." (Eph. 6:4) To the other church, he wrote: "Fathers, provoke not your children to anger, lest they be discouraged." (Col. 3:21) The strong language that Paul used signifies the seriousness of the problem of abuse and misuse of scriptures to justify it. Paul obviously knew the serious consequences child abuse. His term "wrath" means in modern English "enrage." A parent, a citizen, a school official, law enforcement, and judicial personnel do not have to look far to see that an extraordinary number of children are "enraged" in our society. Many of the most violent people among us are children.

The other term Paul used—"discouraged"—in modern language means "spiritless, disheartened, dismayed." These personality traits clearly point to what is now identified as depression. Depression is a serious illness that can progress to severe acts of violence and eventually advance into psychopathic behavior.

The Bible also says: "Lo, children are an heritage of the Lord: and the fruit of the womb is his reward." (Ps. 127:3) Children are a gift from God and parents have a responsibility to both God and their children to rear them according to God's will and direction.

When parents fail their responsibilities to their children, both the parents and the children pay an awful price! The Bible says: "The rod and reproof give wisdom: but a child left to himself bringeth his mother to shame." (Prov. 29:15)

"Even a child is known by his doing, whether his work be pure, and whether it be right." (Prov. 20:11) Children's behavior clearly displays the character of the parents.

Children also have obligations and responsibilities. The

Bible says: "My son, hear the instructions of thy father, and forsake not the law of thy mother." (Prov. 1:8)

Over the last century the legal reformists realized that children were immature and lacked judgment. This led to the establishment of the juvenile court system. It took another sixty plus years for the Supreme Court to realize that the system was a failure.[8]

In the meantime, social scientists, including sociologists, psychologists, and others have conducted study after study, published paper after paper, and wrote book and book addressing the problems of juveniles and the problems. They have linked juveniles' problems with poor parenting, poverty, homosexuality, etc. But not a single study that I have located has ever linked a problem of a juvenile to having attended a Bible believing church. All the time that the social scientists have spend—at the very least--tens of millions of dollars searching for the answer to the juvenile problems, the answer has been right under their noses in God's Holy Word.

Try as they might, the social scientists cannot reinvent God's creation and make it better than he did. He created man in his image and his likeness; and then he told man how to behave.

Parents have obligations to their children and are responsible for their children's guidance. The parents' obligations and responsibilities go beyond providing food and shelter. They also include religious training and teaching.

The Apostle Paul said: "But if any provide not for his own, and especially for those of his own house, he hath denied the faith, and is worse than an infidel." (1 Tim. 5:8)

The solution to juvenile problems lies—not with liberal politicians, liberal school teachers, liberals in the states houses or Washington, or the courthouses—but in the homes of America, and in the churches. I am well aware that not all churches are good, Bible believing and teaching ones, but I believe that at least one good one can be found in every city and community of America.

CHAPTER FOURTEEN

SATAN THE DEVIL

Nobody has ever lived on this earth that has not been affected by Satan the Devil, including Jesus Christ. Had it not been for Satan the Devil, Jesus Christ would not have needed to come to this earth and die on the cross, and not a single baby would have ever died. Satan the Devil brought death to this earth.

Christ came to this earth to offer himself as a sacrifice for the forgiveness of man's sins. But for Satan the Devil's deceptive doings, man would have never sinned.

Satan came to Eve in the psyche of a snake—howbeit as a beautiful snake. He can also be in the psyche of "an angel of light." (II Cor. 11:14)

Satan the Devil is an adversary of everything good and right. That is why that no matter what anybody does that is good and right in the sight of the Lord, somebody is always waiting to find fault and to criticize. It does not matter if he is a good Bible believing preacher or an honest businessman, politician or whoever, somebody will always be ready to criticize and find fault.

However, it is never wrong to criticize sin and sinners. There is a vast difference between criticizing sin and fault finding. Satan is not in the business of finding fault with sin or sinners, but he does love finding fault with God's people.

Satan the Devil acting through the Pharisees found fault with the teachings of Jesus Christ. It was Satan the Devil acting through the Romans that found fault with the teachings of the Apostle Paul.

It is Satan the Devil acting through the hearts and minds of liberals and the ungodly that opposes the teachings of Jesus Christ and the Bible being used in our public schools.

It is Satan the Devil acting through rap artists and rock stars that are misleading the youth of our nation into a life of entertainment that is very destructive. Rap artists and rock stars are the ministers of Satan the Devil and they are preaching his damnable message to the youth of America.

Satan the Devil is also the "prince of this world." (John 14:30) Satan the Devil has control of this world. It is easy to see his influence everywhere. He offers people everything to follow him. One of his main tools is the pursuit of wealth and money. Everybody knows that almost everyone will say or do anything for money. They will forsake worship on Sundays to work for money. They will lie and steal for money. They will drive wedges between family members for money. They will sell illegal drugs and alcohol to anybody for a few dollars knowing full well that it will ruin the lives of the users. Too many people love money too much.

Satan the Devil is a powerful being. (Eph. 2:2) No man can stand against the devil and win except he has the spirit of God in his soul. He is too powerful. He was too powerful for Adam and Eve to stand against, and he is too powerful for mankind today. That is why all mankind have sinned.

Several ministers have said in recent times that "sin will take you further than you want to go, keep you longer than you want to stay, and cost you more than you are willing to pay." Sin will also do something else: it will take souls to hell and cost lives. All alcoholics began with a first drink. They were not born alcoholics. The first drink took them further than they wanted to go. When they realized that their lives were ruined and their health was gone, they had gone further than they wanted to go. When it had cost them their families and their futures, it had cost them more than they were willing to pay.

Satan the Devil is the "ruler of darkness." (Eph. 6:12) Satan the Devil will never come out in the open and tell a young person that the first drink of alcohol or the first use of an illegal drug will be the ruin of their life. He did not tell Eve that she would bring death to the whole world by eating the forbidden fruit. Like a snake in the darkness of night, he will inch his way in and slowly but surely ruin the lives of those which are deceived by him. He will make the young person believe that it is all just fun and games. Nothing to be alarmed about—nothing to be alarmed about at all.

Satan the Devil is "wicked." (1 John 2:13) Wickedness is on every hand. Wickedness comes in many forms. It may be the murderer in the community, the child rapist, the illegal drug dealer down the street, or the false prophet preaching a false gospel to uninformed people, or the trouble maker in the local church. The wicked one may be the politician lying his way into public office—and we have all seen enough of that. He may be a local pastor willing to preach what his congregation wants to hear rather than the truth.

Satan the Devil is a "subtle" being. (II Cor. 11:3) He is smart and clever. There is not a doubt in my mind that there are people who believe that they are doing the will of God when, in fact, they are doing the will of the Devil. The Apostle Paul wisely advised his followers to "put on the whole armour of God" in order to "stand against the wiles of the devil." (Eph. 6:11) He advised the Christians to prepare for war with the devil as a warrior preparing for battle—girt your lions with the truth; wear a breastplate of righteous; shoes of the gospel of peace; a shield of faith; a helmet of salvation, and the sword of the spirit. (Cf. Eph. 6:12–17) Satan the Devil is a warrior and he will fight for every soul until the day he is cast into hell.

Satan the Devil is not only seeking to deceive and mislead the unsaved, but he seeks to mislead and deceive the Christians, too. Christ referred to him as a sower of "tares among the wheat." (Matt. 13:25) And as a "wolf" that "scattereth the sheep." (John 10:12) Peter referred to him "as a roaring lion, walketh about, seeking whom he may devour." (1 Pet. 5:8) Satan the Devil cannot win over God's children because Christ said,

"My sheep hear my voice, and I know them, and they follow me: And I give unto them eternal life; and they shall never perish, neither shall any man pluck them out of my hand." (John 10:27—28)

Satan the Devil is a "tempter." Just because he cannot win over God's people, in no wise means that he does not try. And it may appear that he does win for a season. He tempted David and David failed for awhile (1 Chr. 21:1), but he repented and moved on with his life. He tempted Christ (Matt 4:3—10), and Christ rejected his temptation.

Satan is still an expert at temptation. Not long ago I heard a wonderful preacher of the gospel say that Christians were the worst people to eat their own. All it takes is one little mistake, one little misdeed by a Christian and he becomes the talk of the community. The Christians are the first to jump on the band wagon. They act as if they have never made a mistake or done anything wrong.

There is a wonderful lesson to be learned from the Apostle Paul in this regard. It is a lesson I've never heard a preacher preach on. Paul had heard something. He did not repeat the rumors—he was too smart to do that. However, it had come to his attention that one of his fellow servants of Christ—a brother in Christ—owed a debt that he could not pay.

Onesimus had been involved with Paul's "brother" Philemon. Maybe Onesimus had been a slave or an employee of Philemon. Anyway, Onesimus had departed from Philemon and went to Rome. At Rome Paul had led him to salvation.

Paul sent Onesimus back to Philemon with a letter telling Philemon of Onesimus' conversion and told him Philemon that if Onesimus "hath wronged thee, or oweth thee ought, put it on mine account; . . . I will repay it: albeit I do not say to thee how thou owest unto me even thine ownself besides." (Phil. 1:18—19)

The Bible is silent on the repayment of the debt, but I expect it was forgiven and not charged to the Apostle Paul's account.

It appears that the Apostle Paul did not want Philemon to forget that he owed his soul's salvation to him and implied that that was good reason to forgive Onesimus' debt.

This letter is a remarkable example of the way Christians fellowship and brotherly love should be practiced. It is a certainly that Satan the Devil did not inspire Paul to write this letter. This letter is not a work of the Devil.

The Apostle Paul was a very wise man. He knew the will of God; he knew the law, and he also knew the Devil. In all or almost all of his letters to the churches he warned the Christians to be on guard against the Devil.

In his second letter to the Corinthians he warned them to be on guard against Satan's desire to corrupt the simplicity of the gospel of Christ. (Cf. II Cor. 11:3) It is easy to see the work of the Devil manifested in our country today. We see it in two major ways:

One, there is a vast number of people who believe that being a good moral person will get them into heaven. Others will say that they have never done anything wrong.

And secondly, there are those that say one must do this or that to be saved. Many of these things relate to the law God gave Moses and they constitute a form of bondage that man cannot live up to. Others are forms of self-righteousness. Nevertheless, they work to Satan's advantage and corrupt the simplicity of the Gospel of Christ.

Satan wants people to believe that good works will get them into heaven. The Bible clearly teaches that the children of God will be rewarded according to their works (Cf. Matt. 16:27), but nowhere in the Bible is there the slightest suggestion that good works will ever suffice for salvation. However, this false and misguided theology works well to Satan's advantage.

When the Apostle Paul went to Athens he went into one of the most deceived and misguided cities on earth. It was a totally pagan city. It was a city of unhappy people. They were obviously seeking peace via philosophers telling and seeking new things. The city had many idols—including one to "THE UNKNOWN GOD." (Acts 17:23)

We see a lot of this sort of behavior in the world and particularly in the West today. The news outlets are well documented with new ideals for peace in the world. The problem with all of the new ideals is that they are not founded upon the Bible and the righteousness of God. The leaders of the western world today are being led by Satan and not by God. Consequently the world is headed down a road that leads to absolute disaster.

When the Apostle Paul went into Rome he was very bold in describing its sins and their consequences. For example, he said, "professing themselves to be wise, they became fools." (Rom. 1:22) He condemned them for "worshiping the creature more than the Creator." (Rom. 1:25) The city of Rome had also sunk deep in homosexuality and other sinful behavior. (Rom. 1:25—31)

Not long ago one of the world's best known practicing homosexuals suggested that the root of the world's problems was organized religion and suggested that it should be banned. [9]

If a Christian minister condemns homosexuality he is tagged a homophobe or bigot or worse. It is always acceptable for Satan followers and sinners to condemn God's worshipers and the followers of Christ. But it is never acceptable to the Christianphobes and theophobes to have their sins exposed for what they are.

Satan is opposed to righteousness. He does not want the world to know the benefits of righteousness. "Righteousness exalteth a nation: but sin is a reproach to any people." (Prov. 14:34) "And he shall judge the world in righteousness, . . ." (Ps. 9:8)

God will set in judgment of all people and the Christians will be rewarded according to their works and the unbelieving, sinners and ungodly will be judged according to the law.

God loves all people. He gave his crown jewel of heaven, his only begotten son Jesus Christ to die a most painful death so that the world could be saved. God does not love sin but he loves the sinner. God does not wink at sin, but commands all men to repent. It is his will that all be saved.

CHAPTER FIFTEEN

AFTER THOUGHTS

I have intentionally shied away from current events because I want this book to remain modern and current for all time. The Bible is as modern and current today as it were thousands of years ago. It has not become and shall never become outdated. On the other hand, news and current events are only news for a brief period of time and then become history.

This chapter will, in large measure, be about current events. I am well aware of the ease of associating certain passages of scripture with current events and time often proves those associations to be erroneous. There are reasons to believe that the apostles believed that Christ would return during their lifetimes and now a couple of thousand of years later he still has not returned. The delay certainly does not mean that he will not return. He surely will!

Christ told Peter "upon this rock I will build my church. . ." (Matt. 16:18). Therefore, it is clear that one of the purposes of Christ coming into this world was to establish his church, which has been here ever since.

The best of intentions can and often are wrong. However, considering the milestones of the church and the things spoken of by Christ and history, certain conclusions can be rationally and logically drawn.

First, it is clear that Peter and Paul were the apostles choosen to take the gospel to the West (Acts 20:2 and Gal. 2:11); first to Greece and then to Rome. According to Acts 16:14 a lady named Lydia was the first European converted to Christianity.

Secondly, I believe—but cannot prove—that the Europeans are the descendants of Ephraim and Manasseh.

And thirdly, I believe that America is a God established country given to the descendants of Manasseh and Ephraim to take the gospel of Christ to the world.

To get to the point of what I believe and why I believe what I do, one prophecy concerning Manasseh and Ephraim is found in Genesis 48. Manasseh and Ephraim were the sons of Joseph and the grandsons of Jacob.

God appeared unto Jacob and told him that "I will make thee fruitful, and multiply thee, and I will make of thee a multitude of people; and I will give this land to thy seed after thee for an everlasting possession." (Gen. 48:4)

When the prophet Jeremiah came along, his first prophecy was directed to the "house of Jacob, and all the families of the house of Israel." (Jer. 2:4) Jeremiah denounced the evil deeds of the people. His prophecies sound remarkable like the history of America and the West. For example, the many hardships the children of Israel suffered in Egypt and how they were brought into "a plentiful country, to eat the fruit thereof and the goodness thereof" (Jer. 2:7) is much like the people seeking religious freedom came to America. I believe it is an undeniable fact that America was the country given to a people to promote the gospel of Jesus Christ to the world. And in the face of many difficulties, it has achieved that end. To this day America is doing more to get the gospel of Christ to the world than any people has done in the history of the world.

It is undeniable that America and the West have been the most God blessed peoples of all world history. They have had their troublesome times as well. They have stood against evil at great costs. Prime examples are World Wars I and II. America and the West have also engaged in their share of evil deeds as well. Two evils that readily come to mind are the liquor trade and slavery.

In large measure, America and the West have done their

evils deeds without serious consequences except for the wars. It appears that America and the West have "gotten away" with a lot of evil deeds. It seems that Americans and the people of the West believe that they are exempt from God's laws, word, and warnings. They are not! Therefore, I believe that America's and the West's pay day has arrived.

God's law says that we "shall have no other gods before me." (Ex. 20:3)

America and the West have long put the love of money and the pursuant of wealth of this world ahead of the worship and honor of God. America and the West have become countries of idol worshipers. It seems that America and the West have forgotten that God's word says he "is not mocked" (Gal. 6:7); that "all nations that forget [him] shall be turned into hell" (Ps. 9:17); that he "is the same yesterday, today and forever" (Heb. 13:8); and that "the wages of sin is death." (Rom. 6:23).

Today America is paying a price for gross national sins. For example, we have millions of citizens from other counties in our land. This fact is posing a direct threat to our national security. However, the greed of corporations seeking lower wage laborers want them here. And it is a fact that the corporations and farmers need the illegals here to work. The number of legal and illegal peoples of other countries needed here to work fairly equals the number of future American citizens that have been aborted.

We keep hearing of figures of between twelve and twenty million people being here illegal. Since abortion became legal in 1973, Americans have reportedly aborted approximately 1.3 million babies per year. Those aborted between 1973 and 1992 would now be adults in the workplace. During this nineteen year period, at 1.3 million abortions per year, indicates that twenty-four million and seven hundred thousand Americans have been aborted that would be of adult age today. Without the evil of abortion, the corporations and farmers would not need the citizens of other countries here.

Abortion has also affected the politics of America. Reportedly abortion has reduced the Democratic block of voters by four percent and the Republican block by two percent.

Abortion has cost the American people in others ways as well. The American taxpayers are covering the cost of the illegals' medical care, children's education, judicial services, security measures, etc.

Another serious national evil is the love of money and the pursuant of it. I do not believe that it is wrong to seek wealth or to have money. It is America's and the West's medium of exchange. However, when the love of money and seeking it in unfair, dishonest, and greedy ways is the main purpose of a person's life, it is not good. Some of the most righteous living people I have ever known have been men and women of means. Some of the most righteous men of the Old Testament times were men of great wealth; however, their wealth took second place to their dedication to God.

As I recall when I was a child, I knew of several individuals who were tenant farmers who after a few years became land owners. The landlords of those days were more interested in seeing a tenant do well for himself and his family than they were in profit from his hard labor. Today it is exactly the opposite. Landlords want every penny they can get for their property and they care nothing about the wellbeing of their tenants.

When I was a child, the people of the community were far more concerned with what was right and what was wrong then they were with a few dollars. Their actions were clearly motivated by right and wrong and not money.

Today we see little consideration given to right and wrong. Most people's attitude is get whatever and anything they can by whatever means. The love of each other that prevailed in the community a half century ago have in large measure gone the way of yesteryear's generation.

Another national evil sweeping America and the West is the false godless religions. One is the false godless religion of global warming. To the prophets of this false religion, it is the only hope for the survival of the human race. Maybe the world is warming a bit and maybe it is not; however, regardless of the facts, mankind can do little, if anything, about it.

The Bible is clear: God expects mankind to be good

stewards of the earth and his creation. He expects us to dress and keep his gifts to us. However, when people put the love of his creation above their love and dedication to him, they cross the line between the love of God and their love for his creation.

The godless religions sweeping America and the West take different forms. Some are devoted to abortion. To its supporters, it is the most important issue in the world and they will vote for any politician that promises to protect it. To others the issue is the environment. They do not want energy developed or used, water used, trees harvested, etc.—except for their own selfish needs and wants. They want vast areas of the country off limits to mining and other developments. They are clearly preoccuiped with the creation and their pet ideals is their religion.

Collectively, the worshipers of false, godless religions compose a powerful political block of voters. Power hungry politicians cater to them. Consequently, we have a lot of godless liberal politicians elected to high offices.

When any nation or people violate the first of the Ten Commandments and put the worship of other gods ahead of the Almighty God of Abraham, Isaac and Jacob trouble is not far behind.

Violation of God's law is sin. God's laws define sin. The wages of sin is death. Therefore, we know what the consequences of violating God's laws bring upon a nation and people.

God is God and he always will be God. God has not changed and he will never change. History proves that God is serious about his laws being obeyed.

It is easy today to hear a lot about God's love for mankind. It is certainly true that God loves mankind, which was created in his image and his likeness. But God is also a God of holiness, righteousness, and judgment. Righteousness will never go unrewarded, and sin will never go unpunished.

When Jonah rebelled and sinned against God, he paid a price (Jon. 1:12); David was denied building the temple (1 Chr. 22: 7, 8); Adam and Eve were cast out of the garden of Eden (Gen. 3:23); Sodom and Gomorrah were destroyed (Gen. 19:24)

Lot's wife was turned into a pillow of salt (Gen. 19:26); and the rich man went to hell (Luke 12:16–21). Sin has a high price, but sinners have to pay sooner or later.

Today Islam is sweeping America and the West. It is without doubt the fastest growing religion in the world. People are flocking to it in groves notwithstanding the fact that it is a religion of evil and hate. Nevertheless, those who speak out against it are criticized and vilified.

A short while ago Dr. Jerry Falwell passed away. Dr. Falwell had been a strong, condemning voice against sin for many years. Shortly after Dr. Falwell's death, Shanna Flowers, a reporter for *The Roanoke Times*, Roanoke, Virginia, wrote an article headlined <u>The light and dark of Jerry Falwell</u>, said: "Who can forget his hateful post 9/11 rip, blaming 'the pagans, and the abortionists, and the feminists, and the gays and the lesbians' and other left-leaning groups for the terrorist attacks?" In Ms. Flowers view there is a "dark side" to people who stand against sin, and who condemn homosexuality and immorality. She suggests that Dr. Falwell's ministry was less than successful because: "Abortion remains legal, and gay rights are more accepted now than ever."

On the "light" side of Dr. Falwell, she wrote: "He showed how a group of people with a common mission can come together and effect significant change. There are lessons to be learned in that both locally and nationally.

"Falwell's greatest legacy, however, is Liberty University. The school that he built from nothing four decades ago now has some 9,600 students on campus and 12,000 in off-campus programs." She went on to say that: "That's an undeniable tribute to the Baptist preacher."

With evil sweeping America and the West as it is today and the peoples of our lands failing to see the true nature of sin, I believe a quote from Solomon is well fitting: "The flowers appear on the earth; the time of the singing of the birds is come, and the voice of the turtle is heard in our land." (Song of Sol. 2:20) God is still greatly blessing America and the West, we see his greatness and goodness everywhere. However, from the media, liberal politicians, and the American Civil Liberties Union, and other major communications outlets, "the voice of the turtle" is everywhere.

As of this writing, the United States Congress is doing almost nothing that is worthwhile. They are wasting their time on vexatious investigations, trying to secure America's defeat in its war against pure evil, catering to the worshipers of various sects of godless religions in our country. All the while threats against the security of our country are growing.

In many ways America is going down the paths of the Roman Empire. According to history, the Roman Empire went from being the super of the world to being nothing in a single decade. The culprits that destroyed it were immigration and adoption of the barbarians, high taxes, corrupt politics, and excessive spending of money.

It is fairly easy to understand the evil agenda of the corrupt politicians in America today. They want to tax the "rich" and give to the poor. Since there are more poor people in the country than there are rich, the poor elect the politicians that promise more and more government benefits to them. Soon those classified as "rich" are going to include those earning less and less. At the same time the rich are going to seek more and more ways of evading taxes such as moving to third world countries and taking their jobs with them until the economic base of America will truly suffer.

As of this writing, America is importing more and more of its food supply. One of the reasons why is because so much of its corn is being used to produce fuel. The actual amount of fuel produced from corn is insufficient so far as the nation's needs are concerned. A far wiser choose would be to drill for more oil in our oil rich areas and build more refineries for our short term needs and work to develop more nuclear and hydrogen energy for a long term solution.

The root of problems in America and the West is the sweeping spread of two false and evils religions. One is Islam and the other is liberalism, and unless they are stopped, they will lead to the total destruction of the entire world. Both have already led to multi-millions of deaths in the West and beyond. Islam's evil deeds have already been address earlier, so here only liberalism will be further addressed.

The establishment of religion or its support by government is clearly prohibited by the United States Constitution. Notwithstanding this prohibition, liberalism has clearly become the official state sponsored religion in America. According to Ann Coulter as reported in her book, *Godless, the Church of Liberalism,** the godless church has attributes not unlike many mainstream churches. Including Sacrament: abortion; Holy Writ: *Roe* v. *Wade* (the Supreme Court decision which legalized abortion) Clergy: the public school teachers; churches: government supported public school.

The godless churches' chief false prophet is Al Gore. However, there have been other before him and their false doctrines also led to death and destruction. These individuals have means to getting their false doctrines incorporated into the laws of the land. An example is the environmental laws regarding global warming and climate change. Others relate to the banning of chemicals such as DDT. Since the banning of DDT in 1972 to save the birds, at least 80,000 deaths per year have occurred in Uganda alone from malaria and in the whole of Africa the death toll reaches into the millions. It does not matter that there was a total lack of evidence of DDT being harmful. Now forty years later the World Health Organization (WHO) has reported that DDT poses no health risk "when used properly" as reported by the BBC News. So one book, *Silent Spring*, written by a non-scientist drying of cancer, Rachel Carson, has resulted in more than forty million deaths, but we will never hear a practitioner or disciple of liberalism repent for junk science being accepted as factual evidence.

Apparently the foundation—the bible—for the religion of liberalism is the Darwin theory of evolution. One day the liberals have a theory and then next day it is treated as an ascertained fact. But the real harm is the fact that it gives people an excuse to deny the existence of God. Mankind has always believed in some sort of god, sun gods, moon gods, great spirits, etc. The theory of evolution enabled man to become a god unto himself and empowered him to take responsibility for saving the world from himself. It has led to more than a million abortions per year in the United States, the deaths of six million Jews and approximately seven million Christians during World War II, and multi-millions of others around the world.

Before Darwin and his theory of evolution took root approximately one hundred and fifty years ago, the people of the America were a people that believed in God. America was founded by men that had a deep faith in God. There was a time—before Darwinism—when the powers of government of America had faith in God and so publicly stated their faith:

"It is the duty of all nations to acknowledge the providence of Almighty God, to obey His will, be grateful for His benefits, and humbly to implore His protection and favor." –George Washington, First President of the United States

"Before any man can be considered as a member of civil society, he must be considered as a subject of the Governor of the Universe." –James Madison, Fourth President of the United States

"It is not that in the chain of human events, the birthday of the nation in indissolubly linked with the birthday of the Savior? That it forms a leading event in the progress of the Gospel dispensation? It is not that the Declaration of Independence first organized the social compact on the foundation of the Redeemer's mission on earth? That it laid the cornerstone of human government upon the first precepts of Christianity?" –John Quincy Adams, Sixth President of the United States

"The Bible is the best of all books, for it is the word of God and teaches us how to be happy in this world and in the next. Continue therefore to read it and to regulate your life by its precepts." –John Jay, First Chief Justice of the United States Supreme Court

"One of the beautiful boasts of our municipal jurisprudence is that Christianity is a part of the Common Law...There never has been a period in which the Common Law did not recognize

Christianity as lying at its foundation." –Joseph Story, Associate Justice of the United States Supreme Court

"We are a Christian people...not because the law demands it, not to gain exclusive benefits or to avoid legal disabilities, but from choice and education; and in a land thus universally Christian, what is to be expected, what is to be desired, but that we shall pay due regard to Christianity."—Senate Judiciary Committee Report, March 19, 1853

"At the time of the adoption of the Constitution and the amendments, the universal sentiment was that Christianity should be encouraged...in this age there can be no substitute for Christianity....That was the religion of the founders of the republic and they expected it to remain the religion of their descendants.: House Judiciary Committee Report, March 27, 1854

"There is no dissonance in these [legal] declarations....This is a Christian nation."—United States Supreme Court, *Church of the Holy Trinity* v. *U.S.*, 1892, citing dozens of precedents

"Why may not the Bible, and especially the New Testament, without note or comment, be read and taught as a divine revelation in [schools]—its general precepts expounded, its evidence explained and its glorious principles of morality inculcated?...Where can the purest principles of morality be learned so clearly or so perfectly as from the New Testament." –United States Supreme Court, *Vidal* v. *Girard's Executors*, 1844

"Let every student be plainly instructed and earnestly pressed to consider well the main end of his life and studies is to know God and Jesus Christ...."—Harvard's Student Guidelines, 1636

These quotations clearly show what Darwinism has done to America. It has converted America from being a Christian nation to one of being godless. America has paid a price, and shall continue to do so.

I do not wish to be a prophet of dome and gloom. I wish that I could in good faith believe that hope lies in our future. I cannot do that! Every minister of the gospel that I talk to about our social, religious and economic state of affairs share my view that things are not going to improve but are going to continue to get worse and worse. If our interpretation of the Bible is correct, things are only going to decline further and further towards the forces of evil. We do not need to look too far to see that there is a real effort by the liberal left to atheistize America. And this is a sad commentary for Christ's church-country! However, Jesus is still standing at the door knocking and whosoever will let in, he will save.

God's word is still true. When he said he was the same yesterday, today and forever, that is the way it is. When he said the wages of sin is death, that, too, is still true. When he said that people were to have no other gods before him, he meant that, too. When he said that people given to sin would become reprobates, that is also true.

America and the West have largely become reprobate countries. It is acceptable for public schools to espouse Islam, but hide the truth of its agenda. Muslim cleric Omar Bakri Mohammed stated the Islamic position clearly: "We don't make a distinction between civilians and non-civilians, innocents and non-innocents. Only between Muslims and unbelievers. And the life of an unbeliever has no value. It has no sanctity." The liberals who espouse Islam have chosen names for those whom criticize Islam. However, many of the liberals and their supporters would be the first to die if Muslims were given the opportunity.

The future does not look bright for the peoples of America and the West. However, individuals can secure their future by accepting the salvation that Jesus Christ paid for with his blood.

The only hope for America and the West—if there be any hope for them—is the realization of three things: "[T]he wages of sin is death; . . ." (Rom. 6:23); "The wicked shall be turned into hell, and all nations that forget God." (Ps. 9:17) "If my people, which are called by my name, shall humble themselves, and pray, and seek my face, and turn from their wicked ways;

then will I hear from heaven, and will forgive their sin, and heal their land." (2 Chr. 7:14)

The tap root of America's and the West's sin is liberalism, which is based upon the theory of Charles Darwin (Darwinism). Liberalism has become America's taxpayers supported state religion. It must be stopped. So far America is looking for politicians to find solutions for her problems. However, there will be no solution finding politicians until America rejects sin and returns to God.

PART THREE
FOOTNOTES AND SOURCES

FOOTNOTES

1. Coontz, Stephannie, *Marriage, a History from Obedience or How Love conquered Marriage*, Penquin Group, New York, 2005

2. The West is defined as America and to a lesser extent Western Europe

3. *A Century of Islam in America*, IslamAbout.com

4. Evertt Augspurger and Richard Aubrey McLemore, *Our Nation's Story*, Laidlaw Bros. 1960 edition, p. 55

5. *Cohen v. Virginia*, 19 U.S. (6 Wheat) 264, 404, (1821)

6. United States Constitution, Article II, Section 4

7. *Morrison v. Board of Educ. of Boyd County, Kentucky*, _____F. Supp. 2d_____ (E.D., Ky. 2006)

8. *Kent v. United States*, 383 U.S. 541, 86 S. Ct. 1046 (1966)

9. Elton John, quoted in Observer's Music Monthly Magazine, November 2006

SOURCES

1. A & E, *Jerusalem*, A&E.com

2. Catholic Online, catholic.org

3. Collinge, William J.: *The A to Z of Catholicism*, The Scarecrow Press, Inc., Lanham, Maryland, 2001

4. Collier's Encyclopedia, P. F. Collier, Inc., New York

5. Coulter, Ann: *Godless, The Church of Liberalism*, Crown Publishing, New York, 2006

6. Crowley, Roger: *1453 The Holy War for Constantinople and the Clash of Islam and the West*, Hypesion, New York

7. Dome of the Rock, islamicarchitecture.org; Bibleplaces.com

8. Grant, Michael: *The Roman Emperors*, Barns & Noble Books, New York, 1997

9. Heather, Peter: *The Fall of the Roman Empire*, Oxford, New York, 2006

10. Kamil International Ministries Organization,

11. Khaleej Times, 25 February 2007, Khalleejtimes.com

12. Masson, Georgina: *Ancient Rome, From Romulus to Augustus*, The Viking Press Inc., New York, 1974

13. My Way News, March 1, 2007, apnews.myway.com

14. National Education Association

15. Payne, Robert: *The Dream and the Tomb, A History of the Crusades,* Stan and Day, New York

16. Ritter, Gerhard: *Luther, His Life and Work,* Harper & Row, New York, 1959

17. Spencer, Robert: *The Truth about Muhammad,* Regnery Publishing, Inc., Washington, D.C. 2006

18. Spencer, Robert: *The Politically Incorrect Guide to Islam (and the Crusades),*Regnery Publishing, Inc., Washington, D.C. 2005

19. The Franciscans of the Holy Land: christusrex.com

20. *The Lost Books of the Bible,* Testament Books, New York, 1979 edition